CAN YOU HEAR ME?

Other titles by Penny Kendal

PENNY KENDAL

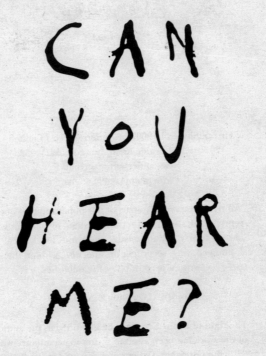

CAN YOU HEAR ME?

ANDERSEN PRESS • LONDON

For Adam with love

First published in 2007 by Andersen Press Limited,
20 Vauxhall Bridge Road, London SW1V 2SA
www.andersenpress.co.uk
www.pennykendal.co.uk

British Library Cataloguing in
Publication Data available

ISBN 978 1 84270 682 4

Mixed Sources
Product group from well-managed
forests and other controlled sources
www.fsc.org Cert no. TT-COC-2139
© 1996 Forest Stewardship Council
FSC

Typeset by FiSH Books, Enfield, Middx.
Printed in the UK by CPI Bookmarque, Croydon, CR0 4TD

Mark

My Earliest Memory

I am two, maybe three years old. My mum is sitting on the floor by the settee, her legs curled under her on the green circle-patterned carpet. She doesn't usually sit like that. Her face is red. She's crying. I crouch down in front of her – bewildered, scared – knowing only that I want her to stop. She doesn't seem to know I'm there.

'Why crying, Mummy?' I say.

She doesn't answer.

'Don't cry, Mummy.'

She still cries. She doesn't stop. I don't know what to do. I reach out – touching the warm, wet tears – trying to take them off her face with my fingers, make them stop. But more keep coming.

Was it me? Did I do something to make her cry? In despair I press my chubby hands over her eyes.

'Sorry, Mummy. Don't cry, Mummy.'

Gently, she peels back my hands, squeezing them tight between her own. When at last she speaks her voice is croaky but soothing.

'It's OK, Mark. It's not your fault. Mummy's OK.'

But tears still come – from her eyes and now her nose too. Anxiously I check her ears. Relief – no tears there.

'Mummy sad?' I ask.

'Yes, that's right,' she sniffs. 'But I'm OK. I'll be OK.'

I wrap my arms round her neck, press my face into the soft warmth of her body.

And I cry too.

One

'This is it.'

Leah had come to a halt by the overloaded skip at the end of the terrace. She waved her arm with a mock flourish towards what she was now supposed to call 'home'. Nikki stopped beside her and stared.

'And you're actually living in *that*?' said Nikki.

'Yeah,' said Leah. She was pleased to hear the appalled tone in Nikki's voice. Her heart sank every time she saw all the scaffolding and tarpaulin, the piles of bricks, the mess – but her mum and dad were acting as if it was normal to live like this.

'D'you want to come in?' Leah asked.

'Er – no – actually, I'd better get back,' said Nikki. 'Maybe another time. Look, if you ever need somewhere to escape to, I'm only two roads down. You can always come to mine. Not that it's exactly quiet.'

'Thanks,' said Leah. She was glad she'd brought Nikki here. She hadn't been sure. She would have liked her to come in, so she could see if Nikki got the same bad feeling as she did from the house. But maybe it was better that she hadn't. Nikki might have thought she was mad.

It wasn't just that it was a building site. Something about the house had given Leah the creeps from the first moment she'd stepped inside. Mum and Dad didn't seem to sense it at all. Dad said it was because she had no vision – couldn't see the potential. She'd love it when it was finished – wouldn't believe it was the same house. He'd sounded so sure, she'd wanted to believe him. It was his 'big project' – buy a decrepit old house and do it up. And he was so happy. It was as if he'd come to life again for the first time since … since what happened. Mum said they had to put up with anything to keep him happy – and she didn't want to hear Leah moaning.

Leah watched Nikki disappear down the road, her long legs making easy strides, hips swaying. She looked far older than fourteen. She was popular too – and the last person Leah had expected to start being friendly. She hoped it would last.

Leah sighed, and stepped carefully along the planks that led to the front door. The way was blocked by a pile of bricks so she slipped through the tarpaulin. She looked up to see her dad perched on a ladder.

'Hi, Dad.'

'Hi, love. How was your day? You should have a hard hat on in here, you know.'

'It's all right. I'm not staying. D'you want a cup of tea?'

Dad smiled down. 'That'd be great. Can you make one for Andy and Dave too? Three sugars for Andy and one for Dave – I think, or maybe you'd better check. They're out the back. Oh – and get them to show you what they found.'

Leah went into the 'kitchen' which consisted of an old corner unit behind some boxes, with a kettle, sink, fridge and microwave, in the dark, dreary room that also served as the lounge and her parents' bedroom. She wiped the dust that had settled on top of the kettle, filled it and switched it on. She didn't mind making tea for Dad but she felt he had a cheek expecting her to be the building-site tea girl.

Out the back, she found Dave mixing cement and Andy sawing some wood. 'I'm making tea – how many sugars?' she asked.

'Thanks, sweetie,' said Dave. 'Four for him, two for me – and not too strong.'

Leah cringed. She hated him calling her 'sweetie'. They were the ones who should be called 'sweeties' with all that sugar.

'Dad said you'd found something,' she added, remembering.

'Yeah,' said Andy. He bent down, revealing rather too much of his builder's bum.

Leah looked away in revulsion.

Dave laughed. 'Pull your trousers up, mate, or you'll get done for indecent exposure.'

Ignoring him, Andy picked up a small object and held it out to Leah. 'See what you make of that. It was down the bottom of that cupboard we pulled out from the back room.'

Leah looked. 'It's a cassette, isn't it?' She took it from Andy's grimy hand, feeling a touch disappointed. When Dad said they'd found something she'd hoped it would be more interesting than this – an old diary, love letters, or a piece of jewellery once worn by someone who lived in the house in the 1930s – for that was when it was built.

She rubbed the dirt from the cassette case with her finger and examined it. It was one that someone had recorded, with a white insert on which was written . . . it was hard to tell, the writing was blurred. Leah struggled to make it out.

TOTP'. That's what it looked like. She opened the case. On the cassette itself, in what looked like a child's writing, were the words 'TOTP 3 March 1979'.

'T-O-T-P,' she said aloud.

'*Top of the Pops*!' said Andy. 'You know – music from the charts. Have you got something to play it on?'

'Mum's old portable CD player's somewhere up-stairs,' said Leah, without much enthusiasm. 'That takes cassettes, I think.'

'Great! You can see what you make of the hits of the '70s!' said Dave.

Leah made tea for her dad and the builders and then made a cup for herself. She took it, along with the cassette and her school bag, upstairs to her shabby bedroom, half of which was filled with boxes of the family's stuff.

She hated this room. The door was dented and didn't close properly. The windows didn't open properly either. As she stepped in, she nearly trod on a CD. She was annoyed because she knew she hadn't left it there. Her favourite music was on her MP3 player and on the PC. It was rare to play a CD these days. Had one of the builders been in her room? She was instantly suspicious – she hated the idea of them messing with her things. She wished she had a lock on the door. But even she had to admit it wasn't very likely that they'd been chucking her CDs about.

The floor vibrated with the 'bang, bang, bang' from downstairs. That was probably it. The floor shaking had jostled the CD from the rack. She put it back, turning instead to the cassette she'd brought up. *1979 Top of the Pops* – she wondered what it would be like.

She pulled Mum's old portable CD/radio/cassette player out from behind a box and plugged it in. It took several attempts to get the cassette in the right way round so that it would play. First there was a lot of hissing and no music at all but then the music started. It was not a good recording – or maybe it was just because it was old.

'Bat Out of Hell'...Yuck. She recognised that one from the radio. She pressed fast forward and tried again. 'Can You Feel the Force?' She listened for only a minute before turning it off. The music was vile. Of all the things they could have found...

Leah sat down at the small crowded desk and put on the computer, selecting a Jamie Scott track from her music files. This was more like it. She turned the volume up as loud as possible to block out the hammering downstairs while she attempted to do some geography coursework.

That night, Leah lay restlessly in bed, unable to sleep. The road outside was not a main one and there was little passing traffic at night. But the house itself was never completely quiet. There was the rustling of the tarpaulin, and creaks and groans from the brickwork and scaffolding. The wind whistled eerily through the draughty windows and made the makeshift curtains dance. The creepy sensation Leah felt all the time was far worse at night. She hadn't had a good night's sleep since they moved.

She must have dropped off eventually because she woke with a start. A noise had woken her – she was sure. She glanced at the clock radio. It was 3.12 a.m. She felt her muscles tense as she reached for the light switch. What was it? It must have been outside.

She sat up. As her eyes adjusted to the light she saw something was moving. The computer mouse was hanging off the desk, swinging back and forth on its lead like a pendulum.

Two

Leah stared at the swinging mouse in disbelief, and then turned sharply to the door – almost expecting to see someone standing there. There was no one. The dented door was as near-shut as it ever got. It was a noisy door – she'd have surely heard the creak if anyone had come in or out.

Her skin prickled. There had to be an explanation. Had she left the mouse on the edge of the desk? Had it gradually slid forwards until it went over? No, the mouse had been on the mouse mat, she was sure, well – fairly sure – and the mouse mat was at least five centimetres from the edge.

Could it have been the wind? The window was over the desk but although the curtains were fluttering, there was no way the wind could be strong enough to blow the mouse right off.

How had it happened? There had been times before when she'd heard strange noises – as if a person was walking about. She'd been scared that someone had broken in but Dad promised her that the house was secure. The inside doors to the rooms with the missing wall were locked and bolted.

Leah was very aware of being the only one upstairs. Hers was the single usable upstairs room and even the grotty bathroom was downstairs. She could feel her heart beating fast and she breathed deeply, trying to calm herself down. She wished she could go into Mum and Dad's room, like she had when she was four years old and had nightmares, and they would hug her and comfort her like they used to. But Mum had had enough coping with Dad's nightmares this last year. Leah didn't know if he was still having them since they'd moved. She hadn't liked to ask.

It would be no good going down and waking them. They'd think she was crazy. She could hear them now, saying, 'Don't be daft, Leah! Go back to bed.'

This thought was replaced by a sudden new, frightening one. What if the house was falling down around her – unstable with its missing wall, tilting so that the desk was now on a slope? Was the house going to collapse inwards with them all inside?

She looked around anxiously for telltale cracks in the walls. There were none – no new ones, anyway.

She lay down, pulling the duvet tight over her head, wishing she could wake up in their old house, in her old life, feeling safe.

*

Walking home from school the next day, Leah's sense of dread was even stronger than ever. She'd tried to take Nikki up on her offer but Nikki said she had her maths tutor coming. Leah wasn't sure if that was true – or whether Nikki had just changed her mind. Somehow she didn't trust her. Leah's old friends had drifted away after what happened – they hadn't seemed to know how to talk to her and she hadn't felt like talking to them. Nikki had been different – chatting but not asking awkward questions. Yet Leah sometimes had a nagging feeling that Nikki just felt sorry for her. For that brief moment the day before she'd thought they were going to be proper friends. Nikki had seemed sympathetic about the house. The thought of having somewhere to go after school instead of back there had meant so much – but she shouldn't have believed it. She shouldn't have dared to hope.

Back at home, she was relieved to find her room looking much as she'd left it. There were no CDs on the floor today. While she did her homework, amidst the banging and the dust, the phone rang. Leah waited for her dad to get it but it kept ringing so she hurried down the stairs to answer it.

'It's only me,' said Mum. 'I had a meeting today in Birmingham and I'm on the train. It's running late – I'll probably be back about 8.30. Just wanted to let you know.'

Later and later, thought Leah. Mum was a manager

11

at a charity for disabled kids and she seemed to be working longer and longer hours every week.

Leah took a ready meal from the small fridge and put it in the microwave.

'Dinner in five, Dad,' she called. 'Mum won't be back till about 8.30.'

Later, at around nine, Mum and Dad were sitting together on the sofa bed watching TV when Leah came down from finishing her homework.

'Close the door, there's such draught,' said Mum.

Leah pushed the door shut. The phone began to ring. Leah picked it up.

'Hello?' she said. No one spoke. The line was crackly, hissing. Probably someone on a mobile.

'Hello?' she said again. 'Who is it?'

Amidst the crackling she thought she could hear a very distant voice but she couldn't make out the words.

It sounded like, 'Can you hear me?' The voice was so faint it could have been a million miles away. 'Can you hear me? Can you hear me?' it was saying.

'I can just about hear you – it's a bad line,' Leah said loudly. 'Who is this?'

'Who is it?' asked Dad.

'If I knew that I wouldn't keep asking them, would I?' Leah snapped.

'Here – give it to me,' he said.

Leah handed him the phone. 'Nothing. It's gone

12

dead,' he said, handing it back to her. 'I expect whoever it was will try again if it's important.'

'I'll do 1471,' said Leah, 'and see who it was.'

She put the phone to her ear and listened to the number, repeating it aloud. 'Isn't that your mobile number, Mum?'

'It can't be,' said Mum. 'My mobile wouldn't be phoning all by itself, would it?'

'I'm sure that's your number,' said Leah. 'It's an easy one to remember.' She pressed 1471 again and repeated the number to her mum.

'Actually – you're right. That is my number,' said Mum. 'What on earth?'

'You must have left your mobile on the train,' said Leah. 'Someone's picked it up.'

Mum shook her head firmly. 'No, I wouldn't be careless like that. I'm sure I had it with me when I came in.' She looked around. 'It must be in my bag.'

Dad picked up Mum's work bag from the corner and passed it to her. She rummaged through it frantically and then tipped everything out onto the floor. An assortment of books, papers, make-up, coins, pens, tissues, health bar wrappers and empty crisp packets formed a skewed pyramid on the carpet.

'What *do* you carry all that stuff around for?' asked Dad, raising his eyebrows.

Mum ignored him, spreading the stuff with the sweep of her hand. 'It's not here,' she finally admitted.

'I can't understand it. Maybe someone snatched it from my bag.'

'When I answered the phone,' said Leah, 'it sounded like someone saying, "Can you hear me?" Maybe they found it and wanted to let you know.'

'Unlikely,' said Dad. 'Probably having a laugh. You'll have to call the phone company, Gillian, and report it.'

'Why don't you ring it, just in case?' Leah suggested.

Mum looked unsure but she picked up the phone and pressed in her mobile number. They waited.

'No answer,' said Mum.

'Hang on,' said Leah. She opened the door that led to the hallway and stairs. 'Isn't that . . . ?'

A mobile was ringing upstairs. It was Mum's mobile tune – 'Flight of the Bumble Bee'. Without thinking, Leah ran up the stairs into her room. Mum's mobile was on the desk. She grabbed it and ran down with it, handing it to Mum.

'How could you, Leah?' Mum said angrily. 'I could do without jokes like that after the stressful day I've had.'

Leah reeled back in surprise. 'What do you mean? I wasn't playing jokes. I was in here when it rang, wasn't I?'

'I must have put it down in your room when I popped up to say hello,' said Mum. 'It's redialled the last number I called but it can't have done it all by itself. I suppose you set a timer on it or something. I know you can do all kinds of things with mobiles these days.'

'But you can't do that, Mum,' said Leah. 'You can't set a phone to make a call when you're not there. What would be the point?'

'So you're saying you didn't touch it, are you?' said Mum.

'I didn't,' said Leah. 'In fact, I hadn't even noticed your phone was up there or I'd have told you, wouldn't I?'

'So if it wasn't you, how do you explain it?' Mum demanded.

'I don't know,' Leah admitted. It was weird. There'd been the voice, too, saying, 'Can you hear me?' How was that possible?

'You nearly had me calling the phone company and the police to report it stolen,' said Mum, tutting.

'But I'm telling you, it wasn't me!' Leah turned to her dad, hoping he'd come to her defence.

He shook his head and shrugged, with a 'leave me out of this' expression.

'So no one believes me?' said Leah, angrily. 'Well, I've had enough. I'm going to bed.'

She banged the door hard behind her and started up the stairs. The door slammed and then there was a further bang. She turned to see that it had fallen off its hinges. Her parents were both glaring at her through the empty doorway.

Three

As she reached the top of the stairs, Leah's rage gave way to a terrifying thought. She hadn't been thinking when she rushed up to get the phone – but if the phone had been in her room and someone had made that call, then...what if they were still there? They might have been sitting in her room watching as she grabbed the mobile phone and ran out again.

Leah listened. There was no sound coming from her room. The door was open as she'd left it. She peered round cautiously. There was no one there. She even checked the wardrobe to be sure. She hated this room, this house. Right now, she'd have given anything to go and sleep somewhere else.

Once she was in bed, Leah lay wide awake with the bedside light on, close to tears. It hurt so much that Mum had automatically blamed her. She wasn't one for pranks like that. And Dad wasn't much help. It was as if her own parents didn't even know her.

16

Then there was the phone call itself. How had it happened? If only she could come up with a rational explanation. How had she not noticed Mum's mobile on her desk? Could she have knocked it on her way downstairs, and accidentally pressed something so that it redialled the last number Mum had phoned – their home number? Somehow it didn't seem likely.

She thought about the swinging mouse the night before. Were the two incidents connected? A new idea came into Leah's head. Maybe it was a real mouse...living somewhere behind the desk. It had come out in search of food and had knocked the computer mouse. She couldn't help smiling at the image of the real mouse thinking it had found a friend and perhaps then knocking the computer mouse out of the way in frustration when it didn't respond. Then, today the mouse had come out again and this time had walked over Mum's mobile phone, pressing on numbers. There'd been the voice – but she must have imagined that from the crackling line – unless it was a talking mouse! She smiled again.

Leah wasn't all that keen on mice but she wasn't the kind to 'jump on a chair and scream' if she saw one. She was relieved at finally having come up with an explanation – one that made sense. She would get a mousetrap tomorrow – a humane one, of course. Then she could catch the mouse and present the evidence to her parents who would have to beg her forgiveness for wrongly accusing her.

The next day at school, to Leah's surprise, Nikki invited her to her house.

'Can we go via the shops?' Leah asked. 'I need to buy a mousetrap. I think there's a mouse in my bedroom.'

'*A mouse?*' Nikki screwed her face up in horror, making Leah wish she hadn't mentioned it. The thing was, she needed to get the trap today and the shop would be closed if she didn't go straight from school.

'How can you stay in that place?' Nikki continued. 'I couldn't sleep in a room with mice roaming about. What if one got in your bed while you were asleep and bit you?'

'That's why I need a trap,' said Leah, shrugging.

'I don't know how you can stay so calm about it,' said Nikki.

They stopped in the hardware shop on the way home and Leah found just what she wanted. It was a humane trap like a clear plastic box. You put cheese in it to tempt the mouse and once it was inside, a door came down to stop it escaping.

'Put that away,' said Nikki. 'I don't want my mum seeing it – she'll wonder what's going on.'

Nikki opened her front door and Leah followed her in. Nikki's house was like a dream. It was cosy and bright and clean. It was welcoming – something Leah feared her house would never be. There were toys scattered around but not a hint of dust anywhere.

'Your house – it's lovely,' Leah commented.

'Yeah – well, I guess anything must seem lovely next to yours at the moment. No offence or anything.'

'No – but I mean it,' said Leah. 'I'd love to live somewhere like this.'

'Come and meet my mum,' said Nikki.

Leah followed Nikki through into the kitchen, which was large with light wooden units and a round table and chairs. A cute-looking baby was sitting in a high chair, banging a spoon, and a curvy woman with long dark hair was standing at the sink, facing away from them.

'Mum, this is Leah,' said Nikki.

Leah felt herself shrink back as Nikki's mum turned to face her. She wasn't sure she liked the way Nikki had said her name. It was as if she was saying, 'This is Leah – you know, the one I told you about…'

But Nikki's mum smiled warmly and when Leah met her eyes they were kind and generous, not pitying as she had feared.

'Nice to meet you, Leah,' she said. 'Would you like a cup of tea?'

Leah turned to Nikki, unsure what to say. Would having tea mean they'd have to stay in the kitchen with Nikki's mum and the baby? Leah felt she wouldn't mind this but what did Nikki want to do?

Nikki didn't seem to read Leah's questions in her face.

'Yes, thanks,' Leah said nervously. 'Tea would be great.'

'Nikki told me the house you're living in is being renovated at the moment,' said Nikki's mum. 'It can't be much fun for you. I remember how it was when we had the decorators in here – the dust, the noise.'

'It's not easy,' Leah admitted.

At that moment Leah felt herself being pushed from behind. As she turned, she saw a flurry of dark curls. A little girl, about six years old, charged past into the kitchen, waving an exercise book.

'Mummy! I need you to help me!'

'Not now, Jess,' said Nikki's mum. 'You'll have to wait. I'm feeding Ben.'

The baby banged his spoon on his highchair tray and gurgled as if in confirmation.

The little girl's face creased up. 'You help me, Nik,' she demanded, thrusting the book into Nikki's hands.

'No, Jess,' said Nikki, pushing the book away. 'Can't you see I've got a friend over?'

Jess stared up at Leah, her big eyes full of surprise, as if she hadn't realised Leah was there at all until now.

'Hi, I'm Leah. Is that your homework?' Leah asked kindly.

'Yeah but no one's gonna help me.' Jess's face creased up again.

Leah didn't want her to cry. 'Let's have a look,' she said. 'What do you have to do?'

'You gonna help me?' Jess asked.

Leah looked awkwardly at Nikki. 'Is that OK? Just for a minute?'

'Only if you really want to,' said Nikki. 'She's a right pain – aren't you, Jess?'

'No, I'm not!'

'Yes, you are!'

'Girls! Girls!' said Nikki's mum, coming over. She put two cups of tea on the table. 'Mind that tea, Jess. It's hot. Now, Leah – what are you doing standing there, still in your coat? Nikki – take Leah's coat. Sit yourself down, Leah.'

Leah gave Nikki her coat and sat down, still wondering if Nikki had meant for them to say a quick hello and go up to her room. Jess sat down next to Leah and slammed her book down in front of her. Nikki came back and sat opposite, sipping her tea quietly.

Helping Jess took longer than she had intended but Leah found she was enjoying herself. When she did finally get up to Nikki's room, Nikki was full of praise.

'You were great with Jess. She drives me mad but you were so patient.'

'I'm not used to little kids,' said Leah, 'but she was really sweet.'

'You should be a teacher when you grow up,' said Nikki.

'Maybe.' Leah wasn't so sure.

*

The pain of arriving back at her building-site house after being in Nikki's warm, comfortable home was so great, Leah almost wished she hadn't gone to Nikki's.

Depressed, she cut a tiny piece of cheese and set her mousetrap on the desk before she went to bed.

She woke in the night – at least, she felt like she was awake but she realised very quickly that it was a dream. It had to be. She could hear a very distant voice saying, 'Can you hear me? Can you hear me?' In the dream she got out of bed and checked the mousetrap. She was glad it was a dream because she would have felt very foolish thinking she'd actually checked the mousetrap to see if a mouse was trapped in there calling, 'Can you hear me? Can you hear me?'

The trap was empty. Back in bed (in the dream, of course) she heard the 'Can you hear me? Can you hear me?' again. It sounded a million miles away. Then she thought she heard the voice say, 'It's no use – she can't hear me,' as if it was talking to someone else. There was such disappointment in the voice, that Leah almost felt sorry for it. She sat up (in the dream) and called out, 'I can hear you! I can hear you!' When there was no response she tried again, louder. 'I can hear you! I can hear you!'

At that moment the bedroom door swung open. Leah jolted back in alarm, her head hitting the wall behind her.

Light from the hall shone into the room. Mum was

standing in the doorway, panting as if she'd run up the stairs.

'What on earth's the matter, Leah? Why were you shouting?'

'I... I dunno,' Leah murmured, realising with surprise that she was sitting up, not lying down. 'Must have been a dream. Sorry I woke you.'

'It's bad enough trying to sleep with your dad's nightmares waking us both up,' Mum moaned, 'without you starting as well.'

'Sorry,' Leah repeated. 'I couldn't help it.'

Mum's face softened. 'Are you OK? I didn't mean to snap. I'm just so tired.'

'Yes – I'm fine. Go on – go back to bed.'

'All right. I'll see you tomorrow,' said Mum.

After her mum had gone, Leah put on the bedside light. She stayed sitting up in bed, feeling dazed. So Dad was still having nightmares. He seemed so much happier now during the day, she'd thought he was really getting better. It wasn't true.

She shivered, pulling the duvet up over her shoulders. Then, out of nowhere, the voice spoke.

'Can you hear me?'

It sounded like a boy's voice, distant but clear. Leah jerked back, hitting her head on the wall for the second time that night. She knew she was awake this time.

'Don't shout out or anything – just nod if you can hear me,' said the voice.

Leah felt every muscle in her body tense. She wasn't sure if she could even move her head to nod, or if she *should,* but she did.

She searched the room rapidly with her eyes, finding nothing unusual at all. The voice spoke again.

'Yesssssss! I've done it! She can hear me! You can, can't you?'

Leah nodded again. 'Just about,' she whispered. 'Where are you? I can't see you.'

'Give me a chance!' the voice protested. 'I've only just learned to make my voice loud enough. I can move things too. I haven't got the hang of visibility yet – though it's supposed to be easier than voice.'

The voice faded as it rambled on, so that Leah had to strain to hear the last sentence.

'Who are you? Why are you here?' she asked.

'What are these?' said the voice, ignoring her question. 'I read the labels. They have music on, don't they, like LPs? How do you play them? Do you have a special kind of record player?'

Before Leah could open her mouth to speak, a CD lifted itself from the rack and landed on the bed in front of her.

'It's a CD – a compact disc. You play it in a CD player,' she said.

Leah watched as the CD case opened and the CD fell out.

'It's beautiful – like something out of a sci-fi film,'

said the voice. 'Make it play. I want to hear it.'

'Not now – I'll wake the whole house!' Leah protested.

'The house never sleeps,' said the voice.

'Yeah right – but my parents do. I've already woken my mum once.'

'Well, you shouldn't have shouted. I can hear you whisper. You don't need to shout. You can play the music quietly. It won't wake them.'

Leah found herself climbing out of bed and putting on the CD with the volume very low. She felt weird – a bit mad, but not scared, she realised.

'So that's how it works,' marvelled the voice. 'And this is the kind of music you like, is it?'

'Yes. It needs to be much louder to get the full effect though.'

'It's . . . different – but I think I quite like it too,' said the voice. 'Can you turn it up a teeny bit, do you think?'

Leah turned the volume up very slightly.

'Thanks,' said the voice.

For some unearthly reason, Leah felt pleased. 'Now, will you tell me who you are?' she asked again.

The voice didn't answer.

'Speak to me,' said Leah. Then, when there was still no response, she asked, 'Are you still there?'

There was no reply.

Four

Had she been dreaming? Leah woke in the morning with the strangest sensation. She had what felt like mild pins and needles all over her body. Had the voice of a boy really spoken to her in the night, demanding to be shown how a CD works? She must have been dreaming – it seemed so crazy – but climbing out of bed she checked her CD player. The CD was in it – the one the boy had asked her to play.

He had been there. However weird and unbelievable, Leah knew it had really happened. He hadn't been scary or threatening and yet she had a bad feeling still – a sense of bleakness. She'd known there was something bad about this house and this boy was connected with it. If he was a voice with no body then that meant he was some kind of ghost, didn't it? He was certainly from the past if he didn't know about CDs. If he was a ghost, it meant he must have died – but she didn't want to think about that. She did want to know more about him though. Had he lived in this house? When? Had this been his room?

He'd been interested in her music. Maybe that *Top of the Pops* cassette had been his! She wished she'd been able to see him. If he came back, she would ask him about the cassette and about himself. And he would come back – she was sure he'd come back.

It was hard to concentrate at school. Leah wished she could tell someone but she knew she couldn't. They'd think she was nuts – even Nikki, not that Nikki would even have listened. Leah had rushed up to thank Nikki for letting her come over. Nikki had smiled but she'd hurried off into school without stopping to chat. Maybe she *had* taken offence at Leah spending so much time with Jess.

Later, when they were told to get into pairs in Science, Leah looked hopefully towards Nikki but Nikki turned her back and paired up with Maxine. Leah was left to make up a pair with Chloe who clearly didn't want her around.

Leah pushed away the pain and thought only of the ghost. Would he come back tonight?

He didn't. Not for four long nights. Leah hardly slept – she didn't want to miss him if he came. Maybe he was busy learning how to be visible, she told herself. When he did come, she'd be able to see him. As the days went by, it began to feel less real though, less believable. Maybe it had been a dream after all.

During the day, the noise from the building work

seemed worse than ever. Leah took to playing her music as loud as possible while she did her homework, to block it out.

On the fifth night Leah had succumbed to sleep. She was woken by a tremendous noise. Her CD player was on and the music was belting out at full volume. She came to in an instant.

'I've done it!' said a voice.

It was him.

'Turn it down! You'll wake my parents!' Leah cried, scrambling out of bed towards the CD player, without even pausing to turn on the light.

'How?' he asked. 'I don't know how.'

Leah reached for the volume control. It was too late. As she turned it down, the bedroom door opened. Dad was standing there.

'What on earth's going on?' he demanded.

'Sorry, Dad. I couldn't sleep – I fancied some music. I meant to turn the volume down low but it came on loud by mistake. I'm really sorry.'

'I didn't know you weren't sleeping,' said Dad. 'Are you all right?'

'Yeah – I'm fine. I'm sorry I woke you.'

Dad sighed deeply and turned to go downstairs, pulling the door to behind him.

Leah waited until she heard him reach the bottom of the stairs. 'Are you still here?' she whispered, turning on the bedside light.

'Yes. Sorry about the music. Will you be in trouble – with your dad?'

He sounded anxious – as if he cared, and the anger that had risen in Leah subsided.

'No, he'll be OK about it – as long as it doesn't happen again,' she told him.

'You're right that it sounds better really loud though,' he said.

'Yes,' Leah admitted, 'but not in the middle of the night. I still can't see you,' she added, disappointed.

'I know,' he said sadly. 'I *am* trying. I was totally exhausted after I came last time and that was just doing the voice and moving things. What's this?' he asked.

The computer mouse began moving across the desk.

'It's called a mouse,' Leah told him. 'You use it to make the cursor move on the computer screen.'

'You what?'

'I'll show you if you like but we'll have to be quiet.'

Leah was desperate to ask him about himself but she was scared he'd just disappear, like last time. She thought that showing him the computer would keep him there longer – then maybe she'd get her chance.

Leah sat at the desk and switched the computer on. She could sense the boy watching over her shoulder and it gave her a strange, tingling feeling.

'Why are you living in a place like this when you're rich enough to have your own computer?' he asked.

'I'm not rich,' Leah said in surprise. 'Most people

have computers at home. They're not that expensive. This is an old one, anyway.'

'Old?' the boy laughed.

'About four years old,' said Leah. 'That's old for a computer.'

'What do you need a computer for anyway?' he asked.

'You can do loads on it. Watch this.'

'Wow! It's like a TV,' said the voice. 'All colour – and everything.'

'You can watch DVDs on it,' said Leah.

'DV whats?'

'Like videos.'

'Videos?'

'Didn't they even have videos when you were...?' Leah's voice petered out. It didn't sound nice to say 'alive'. 'DVDs are films,' she carried on, quickly. 'They come on discs like CDs. Look, first I'll show you how the mouse works. Look. This is Microsoft Word. It's for typing – I do my homework on it.'

Leah demonstrated.

'Can I have a go – with the mouse?' the boy asked.

'I don't know – it's quite tricky to control it when you're not used to it,' Leah told him.

'Let me try.'

Leah felt the mouse pulled from under her hand. It moved on and off the mouse mat sending the cursor flying all over the place and off the screen.

'Try to keep it on the mat,' Leah suggested.

She looked from the screen to the mouse and gasped. She could see a hand. It was almost translucent and only briefly visible but it was a hand – on the mouse.

'I saw your hand!' she told him, excitedly. 'I saw it!'

'How?' he demanded. 'I wasn't even trying.'

'I don't know, do I? I wish I could see the rest of you, though.'

'Really?'

'Of course. It's a bit weird talking to a disembodied voice.'

'*Disembodied voice*,' he repeated. He sounded sad.

'But you could tell me about yourself,' Leah suggested. 'Then you'd be more real to me even if I can't see you.'

'What do you want to know?'

'Your name for a start.'

'Tell me yours first,' he said.

'Leah.'

She waited for him to speak. He didn't.

'What's wrong?' she asked. 'Why don't you want to tell me?'

There was silence.

'Are you still there?' she asked anxiously. 'Please don't go – you don't have to tell me if you don't want to.'

'I wish I was alive now,' said the voice, slow and quiet. 'I'd have all these things too – the DVs and the

CVs and a computer and one of those phone things. That was amazing! I thought it was a calculator until I pressed the buttons and I could hear the ringing and then someone was talking to me. I'd have all these things like you.'

Leah felt her heart wrench. 'I'm sorry,' she said. 'It must be hard...I shouldn't keep asking you questions about yourself. I'm interested, that's all. How about I show you a game on the computer?'

'A game? What – like Pong? Can you play Pong on this?'

'Pong?' Leah repeated. 'What's that? Sounds like a bad smell.'

'It's a Ping-Pong game – like table tennis. We used to connect it to the telly.'

'No – I don't have that one,' said Leah. 'But wait till you see this. Do you think you could use the controls?'

'I can try.'

It took a while for the boy to master but he was so excited when Leah showed him the game that she persevered patiently and even pretended to be hopeless at joystick control herself. While he was playing, Leah kept glancing at the joystick to see if she could see his hand but it didn't become visible again. Gradually he got the hang of it and even beat her once when she was trying her best.

He let out a cheer so loud Leah nearly fell off her chair.

'Shhh,' she said crossly. 'You'll wake my parents, remember?'

'Sorry, sorry,' he whispered. 'I didn't know I could make a sound that loud! It's just that this is fantastic,' he added. 'How does it work? It's like a cartoon only better and you can make the characters move and everything. It's unbelievable.'

'I don't know how it works,' Leah admitted.

'Can we play again?' the boy asked.

Leah yawned. This was all very well but she had to sleep sometime before morning. She looked at her bedside clock. It was 3.23 a.m.

'Only if you tell me one thing,' she said.

'What?'

'Did you used to live here – in this house?'

''Course I did. I can't come back just anywhere, can I? I wish I could. Then it would be anywhere but here.'

Leah felt a sharp pang of disappointment. So he'd rather be anywhere than here with her.

'I've been wanting to come for ages,' he said. 'I wanted to know what things were like now but I wasn't sure if it was a good idea, coming back.'

'You weren't happy here, then?' she asked.

'Why? Are you?'

'Not exactly. Hey – was this yours?' Leah opened the drawer where she'd put the *Top of the Pops* cassette and took it out.

She felt it being pulled out of her hand. It waved

33

around in the air for a moment as if he was examining it. Then it suddenly dropped to the floor, and there was a crack as the old plastic case broke apart.

Leah picked it up, trying to push it back together but the brittle plastic had snapped. She held it out, assuming he had dropped it by accident. 'Was it yours?' she asked again. 'One of the builders found it downstairs. I did listen to a bit of it but to be honest I wasn't that keen. What music were you into?'

There was silence.

'Speak to me,' Leah pleaded. 'Don't go yet.'

But he'd gone.

Mark
My Happiest Memory

It is Simon's birthday party. Simon is my best friend. He is five and has caught up with me as my fifth birthday was in May. I don't want to remember <u>my</u> birthday. But Simon's birthday is different. He lives a few streets away but I'm not allowed to walk there on my own. When I'm bigger I will.

It is July and it's hot. I am wearing my purple shorts, my T-shirt with a smiling sun on it, and my sandals. The birthday party is in Simon's garden. Simon's dad is organising it. I like him. He is really funny — not like my dad at all. We play Musical Statues and Pass the Parcel and we do the 'Hokey Cokey'. Then we play Dead Lions and I win. I am good at keeping still and quiet so no one will know I'm there. Dead Lions is easy for me.

The grown-ups sit around on stripy deck chairs and clap when someone wins. My mum isn't there. She went home after she dropped me off. I wish she saw me win at dead lions but I don't mind really.

Then we have tea. Simon calls me to sit next to him at the

table. There are chocolate spread sandwiches and cheese cubes with pineapple on sticks and fairy cakes and iced gems and salt and vinegar crisps. The serviettes and party hats have the Magic Roundabout characters on them. Mine has Zebedee. Then we have jelly and ice cream and then Simon blows out his birthday candles and we all sing 'Happy Birthday'. Simon's birthday cake is shaped like a castle with chocolate finger biscuits all round the sides. Simon's mum made it herself.

After tea we have races. Simon's garden is big and long so there's lots of space. There's an egg and spoon race and then there's a relay race on space hoppers. Everyone is trying to be so fast they keep falling off. I can't stop laughing.

I don't want it to end – not ever. But it does. Simon's mum gives out going home bags with lollipops and fun bubbles and birthday cake wrapped in a Magic Roundabout serviette and each child gets a balloon. The mums and dads who didn't stay come through the garden gate to pick their children up.

I want to stay as long as I can so I don't mind that no one's come for me yet. Simon has opened a tub of fun bubbles and is dipping the wand in and blowing bubbles all over the garden. Simon and I try to catch them and burst them. We bump into each other and I fall over in fits of giggles.

When I get up and look round I see that all the other children have gone. There's just me and Simon and he lives here and I don't – though I sometimes wish I did.

'Who's coming for you, Mark?' asks Simon's mum.

I shrug. 'My mum or my dad. I don't know.'

'Don't worry,' she says. 'I'll phone and see where they've got to.'

When she comes back she says there's no answer. Maybe they're on their way.

I don't mind because Simon is opening his presents and I want to see what he's got. One present is a jigsaw puzzle with a train on it and another is a Mr Potato Head with plastic bits you can push into a potato to make it look like a funny kind of person. I wish I had one of those.

We're still in the garden but it's getting windy and the wrapping paper starts blowing all over the place. I run around with Simon trying to catch it, laughing and laughing. Simon's dad says Simon had better open the other presents inside so we go into the front room.

A little while later I hear the phone ring. Simon's mum comes and crouches down next to me on the floor.

'Mark – that was your dad on the phone. He said he and your mum have been held up. They won't be back until late and he wondered if you might like to stay here tonight. They'll pick you up tomorrow. All right?'

She strokes my head. I try to take in what she's said.

'I'm staying here all night?' I ask.

'Yes – we'll put up the fold-out bed in Simon's room. You can borrow some of Simon's pyjamas and I'm sure we've got a spare toothbrush.'

I've never stayed over at someone else's house before. I don't even think about what my mum and dad are doing – why they

37

can't come and get me. I don't find out about the hospital until the next morning.

I am going to stay the night with Simon. This is definitely the best day ever. I meet Simon's mum's eyes. She looks worried – as if she thinks I might cry. I turn to Simon and grin with delight. Simon grins back.

Five

The exercise book was lying by the skip when Leah got home from school the next day. She only noticed it after she'd trodden on it and nearly slipped. She picked up the book and brushed the gravel off it with her hand. It had a dusty, faded blue-grey cover with the name Mark Hystaff, Maths, and 3B written on it. Leah opened the book. Each page of little squares was filled with sums. There were a lot of red crosses. The date was written at the top of each page. The book went from September 1975 to April 1976.

Leah didn't know, she couldn't be certain – but her gut feeling told her this was his; this book belonged to her ghost boy. Now she knew his name. It was just a shame that the book was a maths book. It would have been so much more interesting if it was an English book, full of stories he'd written.

'Where did you find this?' she asked her dad, inside the house.

'Not sure, love,' said Dad. 'I don't remember seeing it. Ask the others, if you want.'

'If you do find anything – anything that might have belonged to a boy who used to live here, will you keep it for me, Dad?' Leah asked.

Her dad looked doubtful. 'All right. But I don't want you collecting too much useless junk. We've got enough of our own already.'

Leah went out to tell Andy and Dave. She wanted to find out as much as she could about this Mark Hystaff – and if he wasn't going to tell her himself, she'd have to do it another way.

'Exercise book?' said Andy, frowning. 'Yeah – it was down behind that shelving unit we just took out from the hallway.'

'What did you make of that *Top of the Pops* cassette?' asked Dave. 'More interesting than some old maths, I'd have thought. Did you have a listen?'

Leah gave a thumbs-down sign and made a face. Dave and Andy both laughed.

'There was a lot of hissing. That didn't help,' Leah told them.

Upstairs in her room, she put the exercise book in the drawer with the *Top of the Pops* cassette. As she turned on the computer, she suddenly had an idea. How common a name was 'Hystaff'? She'd never heard the name before. She typed it into the Google search box.

There were two entries. One seemed to refer to a

place in Utah and the other was a reference to a 'Jeff Hystaff'. Leah clicked on this one.

Present at the meeting were Dora Grant, Hugh Dennis, Martin Hart and Jeff Hystaff.

Leah read on. What kind of meeting were they present at? It appeared to be something to do with a merger between two companies based in Lancashire. Leah found it hard to understand. She scrolled down.

At the bottom of the page was the company address along with two email addresses. One was for Jeff Hystaff. Leah sat staring at the screen. Could he be related to Mark? Dare she email him to find out? But what if he was Mark's dad? He might not want to be reminded about his child who died. She couldn't tell him she'd talked to Mark's ghost, could she? Anyway, she didn't know for certain that the ghost was Mark. Then again, maybe he'd be really interested to know. Maybe he'd come down and Leah could re-introduce him to his son and they could talk and they'd both be forever grateful to Leah for bringing them back together.

'I think I'm getting a bit carried away, here,' Leah told herself. But she wanted to email this Jeff Hystaff. Even if he confirmed that a child relative had lived here and had died, this would make everything more real. And he might tell her how the child died. What could she say in the email? How could she phrase a suitable question?

'The house,' Leah thought. 'I'll say I'm interested in the history of the house and who lived here in the past.'

She was pleased with this idea and she quickly typed the email and sent it before she could have second thoughts.

She put on some music and lay on the bed, thinking. If the ghost boy appeared tonight, should she show him the maths book and ask if it was his? Or would that upset him like the cassette had? She thought she should be patient and wait for a reply to her email. She checked her messages before bed but there was no reply yet. She knew if the ghost boy appeared she would find it hard not to question him. There was so much she wanted to know.

Later, when Leah was in bed, her mum came to say goodnight.

'We haven't spent much time together lately,' she said. 'I wondered if you'd like to go clothes shopping tomorrow. What do you think?'

Leah looked at her in surprise. It was ages since she'd had any new clothes – and ages since she'd been out with her mum.

'Yeah, Mum, that'd be great,' she said smiling.

The ghost boy didn't appear that night. The next day was Saturday. Leah checked her emails but there was no reply from Jeff Hystaff.

Downstairs at breakfast, Leah sensed something in her mum's expression that said something was wrong.

'What's up, Mum?'

Her mum beckoned to her to come into the hallway, out of her dad's earshot.

'Your dad had a bad night, Leah. He seems really shaky this morning. Would you mind if we left our outing until tomorrow?'

'And what if I do mind?' Leah asked, unable to stop herself from sounding sullen. 'It won't make any difference, will it?'

'I thought you'd be a bit more understanding,' Mum said angrily.

'Have you asked him?' said Leah. 'Have you asked Dad if he minds if we go out for a bit?'

'You know he'll say he doesn't mind. What's wrong with going tomorrow? Why are you so impatient all of a sudden?'

'I was looking forward to it, that's all.'

Mum's face softened and she put an arm round Leah.

'We'll go tomorrow – for definite – and you can help me and your dad today. I think there's some wallpaper that needs stripping.'

'No way!' Leah protested. 'I'm going out.'

'Where?' asked her mum.

'To a friend's,' said Leah.

She was out the door before she had time to wonder if Nikki would welcome her or if she'd even be there. She could think of nowhere else to go. She'd have to take a chance.

When she rang Nikki's doorbell a man opened the

door. Leah shrank back, shyly. 'Is Nikki in?' she asked. 'I'm a friend from school.'

'Yes, come in,' said the man, with a cheerful smile. 'I'm Nikki's dad.'

'Nikki!' he called loudly. 'A friend's here to see you.'

Leah heard Nikki's voice from upstairs. 'What?'

'Your friend's here,' he called again.

'It's me, Leah,' Leah added.

Nikki's head appeared at the top of the stairs.

'Hi,' she said. 'D'you want to come up?'

They sat on Nikki's unmade bed.

After a few moments of awkward silence, Leah asked, 'Do you ever wonder about your house, about who lived here before you?'

'My parents bought it from an elderly couple, I think,' said Nikki. 'What's there to wonder about?'

'Not just who your parents bought it from,' said Leah. 'I mean, before that and before that – the history of the people who've lived here.'

'I've never thought about it,' said Nikki. 'It's not like it's really old or anything. If people had lived here hundreds of years ago that might be interesting. Then there might be . . . '

At that moment, Jess burst into the room and almost threw herself at Leah. 'I thought it was you!' she said excitedly. 'Will you play with me? Please! No one else will.'

'Leah's come to see *me*,' Nikki told her, 'not you.'

Jess's face creased up.

'I like to see you too,' Leah told Jess quickly.

'But she wants to spend some time with me,' Nikki added.

'That's not fair,' said Jess.

'Yes it is,' Nikki argued.

'No, it's not! It's not! It's not! It's not!' Jess's voice became louder and louder.

'What should we do?' Leah asked Nikki anxiously. She could see Jess was going to have a full-blown tantrum any minute.

Nikki shrugged.

'Shall we have a quick game with her or something?' Leah whispered. 'Then maybe she'll leave us in peace.'

Nikki shrugged again.

Jess smiled. Leah was amazed how quickly her expression could change. 'I'll get a game!' she said with delight, and disappeared.

Jess reappeared with a pile of games so high her curly head was barely visible above it.

'Only one game, I said,' Leah reminded her.

'I know. I brought these so you can choose,' Jess said, pouting.

Six

Back at home later, Leah found her mum stripping wallpaper in the back room. Layers had been revealed, with a pattern of pink and purple flowers being the most revolting.

'How did people live with *that* on their walls,' Leah said, horrified.

'It's fashion, that's all,' said her mum. 'We had something similar to this when I was a child. People do whatever's the in thing. Back then they would have laughed at the idea of plain painted walls. It wasn't trendy.'

'Give me a plain painted wall any day,' said Leah. 'Where's Dad?'

'He's sitting in there.'

Leah went into the other room. Dad was slumped on the sofa, staring at the blank TV screen. Leah hadn't seen him looking so low for a long time.

'What's up, Dad?'

He looked up at her, bleary-eyed. 'Why did I start this?' he said bleakly. 'What's the point of it all?'

'You love this house,' Leah reminded him. 'It's full of potential. You're going to make it into a wonderful home – isn't that what you said?'

'I can't be bothered any more,' said Dad. 'And you hate it anyway, don't you?'

Leah felt tightness in her stomach. Much as she hated the house, if Dad gave up now, what would they do? He had to finish it, even if only to sell it and buy something else.

'I'm sure I'll love it when it's finished,' Leah told him. 'That's why you need to keep working on it.'

'I think I've taken on too much,' Dad said, shaking his head.

'Come on, Dad. You can do it – and what's the option? There isn't one. Shall I make you a drink?'

'You're not happy living like this though, are you?' he said. 'And nor is your mum, I know it.'

'Stop it!' Leah protested. 'I don't want to hear you talking like that. I'm making you a drink.'

Leah was sure the shopping trip would be off again the next day but to her surprise her dad seemed to have regained some enthusiasm for the house and was back to work on it.

Leah knew they were on a tight budget but she was delighted when her mum said she could have the perfect-fitting jeans *and* the boots that were in the sale. She wished her mum would buy something for herself too but she insisted she didn't need anything.

They stopped for a coffee and Leah realised how tired her mum looked. She was sure Mum never used to have those deep lines on her forehead.

'Are you OK, Mum?' she asked.

'Yes – of course,' said Mum. 'But how about you?'

'I'm fine,' Leah told her.

They sipped their drinks and avoided each other's eyes. Leah wished they could talk, *really* talk about how they felt, about everything that had happened – but she'd never been able to talk to Mum. Dad had been the one she confided in – and that wasn't an option, not now.

Leah lay in bed that night, feeling low, contrasting her miserable life with Nikki's bright, noisy family. She wished the ghost boy would appear and even called him quietly but there was no sign of him. She'd checked her emails all weekend but there was nothing from Jeff Hystaff. It looked like he wasn't going to reply.

On Monday at school, Nikki handed Leah an envelope.

'What's this?' Leah asked.

'An invitation,' said Nikki, smiling.

'Are you having a party?' Leah asked. She felt a buzz of pleasure. It was ages since she'd been to a party and now Nikki was inviting her. She'd been right to get friendly with Nikki – and Nikki clearly did see her as a friend – or she wouldn't have included her.

'Not exactly…' said Nikki, as Leah tore the envelope open.

She pulled out a piece of card and read it.

To Leah, please come to my birthday party at 'Clown Town' and tea at McDonalds after. Love from Jess.

'*Jess!*' Leah exclaimed.

Nikki was laughing. 'She insisted on asking you. She says you're her friend and she wants you to come. Don't worry – you don't have to. It'll be a nightmare, for sure.'

'No – I'll come,' said Leah. 'I expect I can help or something. I've never been to Clown Town!'

At home, after school, Leah turned on the computer and checked her emails. The name 'Jeff Hystaff' popped up in her inbox. Leah's heart leapt. She'd given up on him – why hadn't he replied sooner? Of course, she'd contacted his work email address so he'd not been there at the weekend. She should have thought of this. She opened the email, eagerly.

'Thank you for your enquiry. Although I am familiar with the address, 29 Redford Way, Finswood, to which you refer, I regret that I don't think I can help you. My cousin Chris Hystaff lived there with his family in the 1970s. Chris now lives in Leaverton but I don't think he would appreciate being contacted about this matter. I will explain and hope you will understand. While living at that address Chris's wife left him, taking their only son with her. He lost contact with the child, something I think he has always regretted. I don't think he would like to be reminded of that time as it will stir up bad memories for him.

I hope you will understand and am sorry not to be of more help.

Yours, Jeff Hystaff'

Leah read and reread the email, trying to take it all in. It was interesting but it wasn't what she had expected. For a start, there was no suggestion that Mark had died – only that his mother had left and taken him with her. Even if he'd died later, surely this relative Jeff would have known. And then, wouldn't Mark be haunting the place where he died rather than where he'd lived previously?

It didn't make sense – unless the ghost wasn't Mark at all. The ghost might not even be from the 1970s. When he came again, she would have to find a way to make him tell her.

She didn't have long to wait. He came that night.

'Can you hear me?'

'Yes,' Leah whispered, sitting up quickly in bed. She had been dozing on and off, but she was awake when he spoke.

'Can you *see* me?' said the voice.

Leah turned on the bedside light, her heart beating fast.

'Yes,' she whispered. She stared, her whole body stiff as a statue, unable to take her eyes off the faint impression of a boy who was sitting on the end of her bed, a lanky boy, about twelve years old.

It was like looking at someone through a mist – a clear human shape but with fuzzy details. As she stared it was as if the mist thinned and she could make out his features. It felt so different, being able to see him. She felt shy and awkward in a way she hadn't when he was only a voice. Now there was the eerie whiteness of his face under the long, dark fringe of his thick hair, the way his eyes were looking back at hers. His mouth was trying to smile but his eyes – there was something hostile in the depth of their darkness. She felt her hands begin to shake.

'Well,' he said, smiling. 'What do you think?'

The movement of his mouth didn't quite synchronise with his voice – there was a few seconds delay before the words sounded. It was creepy.

'I don't – I don't know what to say,' Leah stuttered.

His smile dropped with disappointment and Leah felt a surge of guilt.

'I mean . . . it's great to be able to see you,' she added quickly. 'It feels weird, that's all . . .'

'You're shaking,' he commented, his eyes on her hands. 'Am I really that scary to look at?'

'No, no – I'm sorry.' Leah clasped her hands together. 'Was it hard to do it?' she asked. 'Did it . . . did it hurt?'

'Not hurt – it's just a lot of effort to make it happen, that's all. It's like – like trying to lift an enormous weight. You have to concentrate so hard. I don't know if I'd have bothered if it wasn't for you. I felt like you wanted to see me. You did, didn't you?'

'Yes – yes,' Leah told him. 'Of course I did. Thank you.'

'I'm not doing it for anyone else, only for you. No one else will ever see me – you understand? And I don't know how long it'll last,' said the boy. 'I might fade out after a bit.'

He was fading already, going slightly fuzzy, but she didn't like to tell him.

'Are you Mark Hystaff?' she asked.

She watched his face closely. His eyes screwed up. Was it surprise – because he *was* Mark, or confusion because the name meant nothing to him?

'What makes you think I am?' he asked.

Leah climbed out of bed and over to the desk drawer. She had to pass closer to him and she felt a sudden chill that made her shudder. She hoped he hadn't noticed. She pulled the exercise book out of the drawer and held it out hesitantly. His hands looked far too translucent to actually hold anything. But he took it – and she instantly wondered if he would chuck it like he had the cassette.

52

He looked at the cover and flicked through the book. 'Do you like maths?' he asked.

'No – I hate it,' said Leah.

'Me too.'

'Is it your book?' Leah asked, impatiently.

He put the book down on the bed but didn't answer.

'Do you have an Uncle Jeff?' she tried.

This time she was sure she saw a jerk of recognition.

'Why do you think I have an Uncle Jeff?' he asked.

'I want to know who you are,' said Leah. 'You don't seem to want to tell me so I've been trying to find out for myself. I looked up the name Hystaff on the internet and found someone called Jeff Hystaff so I emailed him and he emailed back saying...'

'Whoaaaa,' the boy held his hand up to stop her. 'You're losing me. Are you saying you've been talking to my Uncle Jeff? How dare you? What gives you the right? And how did you find him? What were those words – inter-jet? Eee-meld?'

'So you *are* Mark Hystaff?' Leah said.

'I didn't say that.'

'You said "*my* Uncle Jeff", didn't you? If he's your Uncle Jeff then that means you're Mark Hystaff, doesn't it?'

The boy hesitated only a second. 'I might be Mark's brother, mightn't I? Uncle Jeff would still be my uncle.'

'But Mark didn't have a brother, did he?'

'Maybe, maybe not. You shouldn't make assump-

tions, that's all I'm saying. You don't know anything –
remember that. Now what's this inter-jet?'

'Inter*n*et,' Leah told him. 'It's on the computer. You
can get information and contact people all over the
world.'

'So how does that work?'

'I'll show you if you like. But first tell me that you're
Mark.'

The boy didn't meet her eyes but he nodded.
'Satisfied?' he demanded.

Leah nodded, smiling. She switched on the
computer and pulled a box off the spare chair so that
the boy could sit beside her. The chill she'd felt initially
from being next to him seemed to wear off after a
moment, to her relief.

'This is the internet,' she showed him, as the
Internet Explorer screen opened. 'You can type anything in this box and Google will find the information
for you.'

'Google? What the heck is Google?'

'It's a search engine. Something that trawls through
all the stuff that's there to find things with the words
you've typed. What would you like me to put in?'

'I don't know.'

'What was your favourite pop group?'

'The *Bee Gees.*'

'I think I've heard of them.' Leah typed it in and
pressed 'search'.

'Here you are, see? This is a list of things about the *Bee Gees.* I'll click on this one. Look – it gives you a list of all their hits. And you can pay with a credit card and download their music if you've got an iPod or an MP3 player.'

'An MP what? I can't believe all this,' Mark said quietly. 'It's like a different language – a different world. Things like this weren't even on sci-fi movies. What about my Uncle Jeff? How did you find him?'

'The same way I found that pop group. And it gave his email address. That's an address to send messages that come up on the computer. I sent him this message.' Leah clicked Hotmail and her sent mail folder.

'And how does the message get to him?' Mark asked.

'Down the phone line,' Leah explained.

'The phone line? That's incredible.'

Leah clicked with the mouse. 'This is his reply.'

She waited while Mark read it.

'But it doesn't make sense to me,' Leah told him. 'I mean – it sounds like he thinks you're still alive.'

Mark made no response and she turned to see – nothing.

'Mark! You're still there, aren't you? Tell me you're still there.'

Seven

'Mark!' Leah repeated. She couldn't believe he'd copped out again and she was angry. 'Just talk to me, please! Where are you? Talk to me! I want to know about you, that's all . . . I'm interested – you can't blame me for that, can you? Talk to me! Please!'

Leah jumped as her bedroom door swung open. Mum stood there. Her mouth gaped open as she saw Leah at the computer.

Leah quickly closed Hotmail. She didn't want Mum seeing Jeff's email.

'What on earth are you doing?' Mum demanded. 'It's 3 o'clock in the morning! And I'm sure I heard you talking to someone.' She looked around as if expecting to see another person concealed somewhere in the room.

Leah felt panic rising inside her. What could she say?

'You're not using one of those internet chatrooms, are you?' Mum asked. 'I've warned you about chatting online. People aren't always who they say they are.

Someone who says they're a fourteen-year-old boy could be a fifty-year-old paedophile.'

'Yeah – I know all that, Mum. I'm not stupid. And anyway, I wasn't chatting online to anyone.'

'All right,' said Mum, grudgingly. 'So?'

'I think I must have been sleepwalking and talking in my sleep,' said Leah. 'I didn't know what I was doing. You woke me out of it when you came in.'

Leah met Mum's eyes very briefly and then looked away. Mum didn't look at all convinced.

'Who did you think you were talking to, then?' she asked.

'I can't remember anything,' said Leah. 'It was gobbledygook, I expect. Go back to bed, Mum. I'm sorry I woke you. I'm fine now.'

'*Sleepwalking*,' said Mum, shaking her head.

Leah held her breath. Any second now Mum was going to say, 'I don't believe that for one minute. Now tell me what you were doing.'

But when Mum spoke, her words were soft, not angry. 'The stress of all this is getting to you, isn't it? I'm sorry, Leah. I wish I could wave a magic wand and make everything better – back to how it was before…'

'So do I,' Leah said wistfully.

'Maybe you should see a counsellor, someone outside the family that you can talk to about everything.'

'No, Mum – I don't need that. I'll be fine.'

*

After Mum had gone, Leah slipped into bed but she realised she needed to go to the toilet. Sighing, she pushed her feet into her slippers and crept quietly down the stairs. She could hear Mum's voice in the front room and paused to listen.

'I think it's affected her more than we thought,' Mum was saying. 'She was talking to someone – but I'm sure there was no one there. Maybe it was him...the boy, you know...'

'I don't get it. Why would she be talking to him?' Dad mumbled.

'She's traumatised, that's why. Like you. It's her way of coping, I guess.'

'But she didn't see...' Dad began.

Leah didn't wait to hear more. She went into the bathroom. A brief image of what she had seen that terrible day flashed through her mind and she pushed it away as nausea rose in her throat. Mum and Dad didn't know she'd seen. But she wasn't traumatised. She wasn't like Dad. She was coping. She was fine.

Back upstairs in bed, Leah pushed all thoughts of that day out her mind and lay thinking about Mark and about Jeff's email. How could it make sense? If Mark's dad had lost contact with him completely, then maybe he really didn't know Mark had died. Leah thought Mark's mum would have got in touch to tell him that –

but maybe she didn't know where he was living. Maybe it was Mark's dad's fault that he hadn't kept in touch and Mark's mum was angry with him and didn't think he had a right to know – or even cared.

But why was Mark's ghost here, in this house? Jeff said Mark's mum had left, taking Mark with her – but maybe it was the other way round. It was a long time ago – Jeff might not be remembering it right. Maybe Mark's dad had left and Mark and his mum had stayed in the house.

As these ideas floated round her mind, Leah became increasingly drowsy, and finally drifted off to sleep.

Mark didn't reappear for the rest of the week. On Thursday after school Leah went to the toy shop to find a present for Jess's birthday. It was fun looking at toys but Leah found it hard to choose. In the end she bought a cuddly monkey.

Saturday was the party. Clown Town was a crazy place, like an indoor adventure playground with slides and ball pools and all the workers dressed like clowns. This terrified one of Jess's friends and Leah found her first job was comforting the girl, who said she wanted her mum and she wanted to go home. To Leah's relief, she calmed down very quickly when she saw the others having fun and she soon disappeared into a ball pool.

'Oh, Leah – can you watch Ben for me for a minute?' Nikki's mum asked.

Leah found herself holding a baby for the first time in her life. He was much heavier than she'd expected but he gurgled happily enough, as she bounced him on her lap. He seemed fascinated by everything that was going on.

'You OK there?' Nikki asked, coming over.

'I'm having a great time,' said Leah.

Nikki smiled, mockingly.

At that moment Ben gave a huge burp and they both laughed.

'Leah! Look at me!' called Jess, from the top of the highest tower.

'Wow! You're the Queen of the Castle!' Leah called back.

'Let's play Hide and Seek!' said Jess. 'We'll all hide and you and Nikki can find us. Close your eyes and count to twenty – and no peeking.'

'But I'm holding Ben,' Leah protested.

'Here – I'll take him,' said Nikki's dad, holding out his arms. 'I can't bear this place. It's a madhouse! What happened to the nice parties like I had when I was a kid – with Pass the Parcel and Musical Bumps? I did offer to do one like that for Jess but no, no – it had to be Clown Town and McDonald's.'

'Leah!' yelled Jess. 'Come on! You're not counting!'

'Sorry – I'm ready now,' said Leah.

*

By the time they had finished at Clown Town and McDonald's Leah was exhausted. Somehow though, she had a feeling she had enjoyed herself more than if it had been Nikki's party she'd been invited to.

Eight

As she walked home along her road, Leah found herself following a skinny, elderly woman who was bent over, carrying an over-full shopping bag. Leah saw in an instant that the plastic bag had begun to split but before she could call out to warn the woman, the entire contents were all over the pavement.

'Can I give you a hand?' said Leah, hurrying up.

'No – no, I'm sure I can manage,' said the woman, tut-tutting at all the mess. 'Look – and the eggs are all broken. I knew I had too much in that bag.'

'I only live over there,' said Leah, pointing to the end of the terrace. 'Let me at least fetch a bag to put everything in – and a rubbish bag for the broken things.'

'That's sweet of you – but my house is just there.' She was pointing two doors further up the road to a house that was nearer than Leah's. 'If you don't mind waiting with the shopping I'll get some bags myself.'

'Sure,' said Leah.

While the woman walked stiffly up her front path, Leah gathered the things on the pavement into two piles – salvageable and beyond use. Would the woman want to keep the tins of baked beans with dents in, she wondered. The dents were only small.

The woman returned, and began bending awkwardly to pick things up.

'Let me do that,' said Leah.

'You're so kind,' said the woman. 'So you live in the end house, then? Lot of work going on there, from the look of it.'

'My dad's doing it up,' Leah explained.

'I should think it must need it,' said the woman. 'It's kept changing hands, that house. No one's stayed long enough to do the work on it. Looks like your dad's up for the task though! I hope you'll be staying a good while.'

Leah cringed at the thought of this, but forced a smile. 'Have you lived here long?' she asked.

'Twenty years!' said the woman.

'That's a long time,' said Leah. She wished it was longer though – it wasn't long enough for the woman to remember Mark. 'Do you know if there's anyone in the street who's lived here longer than that?' she asked. 'It's just that I'm interested in the history of our house. It's for a project for school.'

'Dora Lemming, number 23, she's been here longer than me – must be forty years, I should think. She's a good friend of mine. We can walk down there and I'll introduce you if you like.'

'Thanks, that would be great,' said Leah.

'My name's Anne, by the way.'

'Leah,' said Leah.

Leah helped the woman put away the shopping in the small but tidy kitchen. Then they walked down to number 23.

'I hope she's in!' said Anne, ringing the bell.

But at that moment the door opened. The woman who stood there was as round as Anne was thin. Her front teeth stuck out as she smiled to greet them.

'History, is it?' asked Dora once they were inside. 'I don't call the 1970s history! History was the Romans and the Tudors in my day – not the '70s! Makes me feel dead old!'

'You're right there!' said Anne.

'Do you remember who lived in my house in the 1970s?' Leah asked.

'My oh my! What a memory test!' Dora clutched her head. 'It wasn't Vera and Pete? No, they came later. I think it was Maggie and Chris…Yes, that's right. They had a boy – what the dickens was his name? Mark, yes, I think that was it.'

'What were they like?' Leah asked.

'Nice couple, from what I remember. I think there was some trouble between them in the end – Chris and Maggie. She left with the boy. Chris didn't stay here long after that.'

'Maggie definitely left with her son?' Leah asked. 'It wasn't the other way round? You're sure Chris didn't leave?'

'Yes, it was Maggie and the boy who left – but I thought it was the house you were interested in?'

Leah nodded, embarrassed. 'Yes, the house – but the people too.'

'My Kathy would remember better,' said Dora. 'She used to baby-sit for the boy from time to time. She'd be able to tell you what the house was like inside – that's if she remembers. I never went in there myself.'

'Kathy? Is that your daughter?' Leah asked.

'Yes – look, that's her – see the photo there?'

Leah looked. The woman in the photo on the wall looked about fifty and had the same sticking-out teeth as her mother.

'In Australia,' said Dora.

'Oh – is she?' said Leah, disappointed. If Kathy had baby-sat for Mark, she might be the best person Leah could talk to.

'No – not now! That was on holiday last year. Actually she's due here any minute. She's taking me round there for dinner.'

At that moment the doorbell rang.

'That'll be her now.'

Kathy came in, looking very much like her photo but a lot paler.

'Cor, Mum! You having a party or something?' She smiled at Anne and then at Leah, as Dora explained why they were there.

'Yeah – I remember Mark,' she told Leah. 'He was a sweet kid but a bit of a pain. I don't remember much about the house, though. Downstairs bathroom – but they're all like that. If you want to know about the wallpaper – I can't help you there! Lots of patterns – that was the in thing in the '70s – zigzags and flowers and that.'

'And Mark moved away with his mum?' Leah asked.

'Yes – that's right. When did they move?' She turned to Dora. 'Do you remember, Mum?'

'He was here for the jubilee,' said Dora. 'It's funny – I can picture him at the street party, walking up and down, eyeing up all the food. I think he was a bit overwhelmed by it all!'

'Yes – there's a picture, isn't there, that was in the local paper. That's why you remember it. You've got the cutting somewhere, haven't you, Mum?'

'Yes – but it'll be up in the loft, who knows where...' Dora looked doubtful.

'Don't worry,' said Leah.

'He was certainly at secondary school by the time they moved,' said Kathy. 'I should think it would have been '79 or '80.'

She looked at her watch. 'Come on, Mum. We'd better get going.'

'Thanks for your help,' said Leah, as she and Anne both took the hint and stood up.

'You're welcome – anytime, dear,' said Dora. 'I don't think we've been much help but good luck with the project.'

Back at home, climbing the stairs, Leah thought through what she knew. Jeff had been right about Mark's mum leaving and taking him with her, even though it didn't make sense.

As she entered her bedroom Leah saw straight away that the computer was on. She hadn't left it on, had she? Her foot knocked something on the floor. She looked down. The floor was scattered with CDs as if someone had pulled them out of the rack and flung them round the room. *Someone*...

'I'll kill him!' was her initial thought. But of course, you couldn't kill a ghost.

Nine

'Your dad mentioned something about a cassette,' said Mum, the following evening. '*Top of the Pops* from the 1970s, is that right?'

Leah nodded.

'Have you listened to it?' asked Mum.

'A bit – the sound's not too good – or maybe it's just the 1970s music,' said Leah, making a face.

'What was Number One?'

'I didn't get that far,' said Leah, shrugging.

'Can I borrow it?' asked Mum. 'I'd like to have a listen.'

'Sure – if you want. I'll bring it down.'

Leah took the player and the cassette downstairs to her mum in the front room and plugged it in.

'Don't Cry for Me, Argentina', came on, with a hissing accompaniment.

'You know this one, don't you?' asked Mum. 'It was in the film, *Evita*. This is *The Shadows*, singing. I used to love them.'

Leah slumped on the sofa next to her. 'It sounds vaguely familiar.'

The next song was 'Bat out of Hell' at number 17 in the charts.

'Meatloaf!' cried Mum. 'He was something!'

'And you say my music is a racket!' laughed Leah. They listened on. 'Actually I quite like it,' said Leah.

A song called 'Can you Feel the Force' by a group called *Real Thing* was played next – at number 14. Then 'Lucky Number' by Lene Lovich.

'What happened to all these pop stars?' asked Leah.

'Who knows?' said Mum. 'I think I'll wind it on a bit, if that's OK? I want to know what was Number One.'

Mum pressed fast forward and then play. '*And up at number 4, "I will survive"*,' said a voice.

'Gloria Gaynor! You know this one, don't you?' said Mum.

Leah nodded.

Gloria Gaynor sang on.

Then there was a shout – a man's voice on the tape, competing with Gloria's. Leah sat up, leaning forward to listen. What was he shouting?

'Turn that racket off! How many times do I have to ruddy tell you? Turn it off now!' The man's voice wasn't just angry – it was mean and cruel.

'But I'm listening – and I'm rec—' It was a boy's voice – brief and instantly interrupted – but surely Mark's.

'Off – now!' The man's voice boomed.

'Ahhhh!'

Leah felt herself shrink back at the sound of the boy's cry. The man had hit him – Leah was sure.

The recording stopped abruptly and only the hissing continued. Leah didn't move to turn it off. She was too stunned. As her mum stood up and switched it off, Leah thought about what had happened when she'd handed the cassette to Mark – the way it had hit the floor as if he'd thrown it. No wonder – if he remembered how it ended.

'That was horrid,' she said.

'Not too pleasant,' Mum admitted, 'but the boy might have been driving him mad for ages, playing loud pop music at all hours. I know how that feels...' She gave Leah a teasing smile. 'It did sound like he'd been warned before.'

'But Mum – he hit him, didn't he – at the end? Surely that was going too far.'

Mum made a face. 'I don't think he hit him. The boy probably cried out when he saw his dad was reaching to turn off the radio or TV or whatever it was.'

'He hit him,' Leah insisted. 'That was a cry of pain – not just anger.'

'You can't tell,' said Mum, shaking her head. 'I wouldn't worry about it anyway – I'm sure he survived. I wonder what was Number One that week. We'll never know now.'

Back upstairs, Leah turned on the computer. Idly, she connected to the internet and searched for 1979 Number One hits. If Mum wanted to know what was Number One then she would find out. She was looking for March 3rd, the date on the cassette; the week when Gloria Gaynor's 'I will survive' was at number 4.

It took a few attempts – but she found it. Number One that week was the *Bee Gees*. The song was 'Tragedy'.

Leah leaned back in the chair. Hadn't Mark said the *Bee Gees* were his favourite group? 'Tragedy'. That was ironic – or was it? Mark had died, as a child. That was a tragedy. It must have been, however he'd died. But how *had* he died?

She could hear the man's voice on the tape in her mind. She imagined Mark's father as a cruel child abuser who had finally, in a fit of violent temper, killed his son. As Mum would say, she had a vivid imagination. It couldn't possibly be true. If it was, Mark's dad would be in prison and people like Jeff and Dora down the road would have told her. She didn't know Jeff but Dora seemed like an honest person and she'd said Chris and Maggie were a nice couple. Leah put the thought out of her mind.

'Jess is driving me mad,' Nikki said at school the next day. 'She doesn't stop nagging me the whole time.'

'Your mum's busy with the baby so I suppose she's turning to you instead,' said Leah. 'She's probably jealous of the baby too.'

71

'Fine – *Miss Psychologist* – but what can I do about it? Any ideas?'

'You could come to my place after school if you like,' said Leah. 'It's not exactly quiet, as you know – but there's no nagging little sisters.'

'All right – I will,' said Nikki. 'I think hammering and drilling might make a nice change.'

'Hmm,' said Leah.

After school, up in Leah's bedroom, there was an awkward silence between her and Nikki. Leah put on some music to drown out the banging below but the awkwardness was still there.

'Shall we look up that website for the geography homework?' Nikki suggested.

'Yeah – if you like,' said Leah. The website had been recommended by the older sister of someone in their class.

'Have you got the address?' Leah asked.

Nikki reached into her bag while Leah turned on the computer and they sat down at the desk. 'Sorry it's a bit slow.'

'Don't worry – mine's not much faster,' said Nikki.

There was some good information on the site. It answered all the questions they'd been set.

Nikki smiled at Leah.

'I'll print it out, shall I?' said Leah.

'No need – there's far too much. Let's just jot

down the answers we want. Have you got a pen handy?'

'In that top drawer,' said Leah.

Nikki pulled the drawer open and scrabbled around while Leah scrolled down the web page.

'What's this?' Nikki asked.

Leah looked down. Nikki was holding Mark Hystaff's maths book.

Leah felt her heart give a little skip.

'Just something the builders found,' she told Nikki. 'I think it belonged to a boy who lived here in the 1970s.'

'Is that what got you interested in the history of this house?' Nikki asked.

'Yeah – it made me wonder, that's all.'

'Mark Hystaff,' Nikki read aloud from the book cover. 'I wonder what he's doing now. Have you looked for him on the net? You might be able to find him and email him or something. He could tell you what the house was like when he lived here – if you really want to know.'

'Yeah – I've looked.' Leah explained about emailing Jeff Hystaff.

'So did this Jeff know how you could find Mark?'

'No – he said Mark's dad lost touch with him so his dad's cousin wouldn't know.'

'How old would Mark be now?' asked Nikki.

'I'm not sure,' said Leah. It was weird talking about Mark as if he was still alive when she knew he was dead

73

but she couldn't tell Nikki that without talking about the ghost. At least Nikki sounded interested.

Nikki picked up the maths book and flicked through it. 'I'd have thought he'd have been eight or nine when he did this.'

'So he'd have been born in 1967 or 8,' Leah worked out.

'He must be about forty now – like my dad,' said Nikki. 'It'd be like detective work to try and find him, wouldn't it? Is that what's got you going?'

Leah nodded.

'I wonder what he does for a living,' said Nikki. 'I bet he's not a mathematician or an accountant judging by this maths!'

'Do you want to hear the *Top of the Pops* cassette?' Leah asked. 'There's voices at the end – I think it's Mark's dad yelling at him to turn the music off.'

'Really? Yeah – I'll hear the voices, if you like. I'm not much into 1970s music though.'

Leah played the end of the cassette.

'I'm glad my dad's not like that!' Nikki exclaimed.

'Me too,' said Leah. 'Do you think he hit him at the end? It sounds like it to me but my mum thought I was imagining it.'

'Not sure – he might have done. It's weird, thinking about *that* happening in this house – maybe in this room – all those years ago.'

'It gives me the creeps,' said Leah. 'But it makes me

more curious too. How do you think I could find out more about him?'

'If you've tried the internet, I don't know. That would've been the best bet. Maybe the builders will find something else, under the floorboards or something – that'll give you more clues.'

'Leah felt a sudden shiver. *Under the floorboards.* What if Mark's body was under there? What if his dad had killed him and nobody knew? She scolded herself for these crazy thoughts.

'If I think of any other ideas – how to find him,' said Nikki, 'I'll let you know.'

'Thanks,' said Leah.

Mark
A Day at The Seaside

It's one of those mornings after. I know it, the moment I wake up. I have the aching and that sinking feeling in my stomach. I am six years old. I don't want to remember. Instead, I remember something else. Today at school it is my turn to show my project. I did it on aeroplanes and I've drawn pictures of a jumbo jet and Concorde. I've even made a model of Concorde out of plasticine. I get up, excited and eager to get to school.

Soon I am dressed in my school uniform and ready to go downstairs. Daddy will have left for work already and I can hear Mummy in the kitchen. As I reach the kitchen door, I freeze. Daddy is in the kitchen. I can only see his broad, brown-shirted back. He is sitting at the kitchen table. Why isn't he at work?

He hears me and turns. I swallow hard. He is smiling. I am instantly suspicious.

'Back upstairs, you,' he tells me.

I frown, confused. What have I done now?

'Out of that uniform – no school today. I've got other plans.'

I'm still frowning.

His smile grows bigger.

'We're going to the seaside!' he announces.

'But I've got to go to school,' I say. The words slip out before I can stop them. I want to explain about my project but his face silences me.

It can do that, his face. It's always amazed me how the eyes and mouth can move so slightly and change his normal human face into one of a monster, with eyes that are almost popping out of his head and a mouth that looks like it could eat you in one bite.

'What kid would rather go to school than to the seaside?' he sneers, but his voice quickly softens again.

'Are you worried what the teacher will say?' he asks, not waiting for a reply. 'No need. Your mum will write you a note tomorrow – say you had a tummyache. You won't get in any trouble. It's a special treat, this – a day at the seaside, you, me and your mum. We'll have a lovely time, won't we?'

I nod but those last words sound more like a threat to me. I know what this is – it's to try and make up for what happened yesterday. This is what he does. He thinks a treat will make everything OK but it won't. I look at Mummy in desperation. Does she want to go to the seaside? She's washing up at the sink. She doesn't look round. I think she must've forgotten about my project. If I miss my turn, Miss Pinkham might not give me another one, or I might have to wait until after everyone else and that will be like forever.

'Off you go then,' says Daddy.

I look at him – for a moment almost believing he's realised – and he's going to let me go to school. But he means go and get changed.

I go.

It's cold and windy at the seaside. It's not even sunny but Mummy is wearing her sunglasses anyway to pretend. We sit shivering on beach towels. Well, I'm shivering and I can see Mummy is too. Daddy never seems to get cold. No one else is on the beach. Daddy has bought me a bucket and spade so I feel like I have to build a sand castle. I fill the bucket with sand, pat it down and turn it upside down. At first it won't come out so I tap it hard and the sand comes out in a mound that slides away to almost nothing.

'Give it here,' Daddy says, snatching the bucket. 'You need to dig deeper to get to the wet sand. Then it will hold together like this.'

Daddy's sand castle is perfect. I try again, nervous as he's watching me. My second effort is better than my first but Daddy is tut-tutting.

'Why don't we walk along the prom a bit,' Mummy suggests quietly.

I hope he'll say yes – walking will be much better than sitting like this.

'Yes,' says Daddy, cheerfully. 'We'll get some ice creams.'

'Not for me, thanks,' says Mummy.

I want to say, 'Not for me either,' but somehow I daren't.

'Here, Mark – they've got ninety-nines – your favourite,' says Daddy.

My stomach is churning. I take the ice cream reluctantly. Daddy's face begins to turn monsterish.

'Thanks,' I add quickly, forcing a smile.

He smiles back. I notice he doesn't buy an ice cream for himself.

I hold my ice cream cornet and it feels like a lead weight. I slow down so that I am behind Mummy and Daddy. I don't know what to do. I know I can't eat it. I'll be sick. I already feel sick just looking at it. At least it's not melting too fast like it would if it was hot and sunny. But I can't just drop it or he'll see. I can't walk with it forever and I can't carry it home in the car.

At that moment there's a flurry of something over my head and a flash of white in front of my face. I duck – I don't know what's happening but then I see. It's a gull – a huge seagull and it's dived down from the sky and tried to grab my ice cream. I'm left holding the bottom of the cornet and the rest is splattered on the prom.

Mummy and Daddy have turned round. I panic – what's he's going to say?

But he's laughing. 'Must've been a hungry one, that seagull!' he laughs. 'The cheek of him! Don't worry, Mark, I'll get you another.'

My heart sinks. 'No – it's OK,' I say. 'I'd eaten most of it.'

I hold my breath. I don't think you can tell from the splatter on the ground how much there was.

'All right – if you're sure,' he says.

There is a shrill cry from above. I look up. The seagull is perched on a post, looking down.

I give him a huge smile of thanks.

Ten

'You'll never guess,' said Nikki, at school the next day. She was looking excited, her eyes wide and sparkly.

'What?' Leah asked. 'Has Jess stopped nagging you or something?'

'No – I wish!' said Nikki. 'It's not to do with Jess. It's that Mark Hystaff you were on about.'

'Oh?' Leah looked at her in surprise.

'I mentioned his name to my dad – you know, with him being the same age and that. You won't believe this – your Mark was only at school with my dad! They were mates!'

'Really?' Leah's voice came out squeaky. She could hardly believe it. 'So what did he tell you about Mark?'

'He lost touch with him years ago – when they were still kids. So he doesn't know what he's doing now. But when I told him your address he remembered Mark living there. He said what you told me – that Mark moved away with his mum when his parents split up.'

'D'you think your dad would talk to me about him?' Leah asked.

'Sure – I don't see why not. I don't think there's much more to tell though. Hey – I know. I could ask Dad to look on the *Friends Reunited* website. Mark might be on that.'

'Thanks. That'd be great,' said Leah. He wouldn't be on it, of course. But maybe Nikki's dad could help somehow.

Mark had not appeared since Leah showed him Jeff's email. He'd had that one angry outburst when he'd chucked Leah's CDs around but since then, there had been no sign of him. If he did come back, Leah decided she wouldn't tell him about her research or about Nikki's dad. Instead, she was determined to keep him happy, to keep him coming.

It was a shock when she came up to her bedroom at nine-thirty that night, to find him lying on her bed. He was on his back, hands behind his head, staring at the ceiling. He was translucent – she could see the duvet through him – but he was less misty-looking than he had been last time. His features were clear. He looked deep in thought.

She felt an instant flash of anger. How dare he? It was her room – her bed. But she did want him to come – so she pushed the anger away. He hadn't seen her yet.

'Hi,' she said quietly.

He sat up. 'I was waiting for you,' he said. His face was serious. 'I hope you don't mind me being on your bed,'

Leah shrugged.

'I used to have my bed round the other way – against that wall,' he told her, waving his arm.

'Did you? Well, I like it like this,' said Leah.

'Listen – I wanted to say sorry – about the CDs,' said Mark. 'I didn't like you getting on to my Uncle Jeff. It wasn't right.'

'I won't do it again,' Leah promised. 'I won't keep asking you questions either.'

They were both quiet for a moment.

'Would you like a game on the computer?' Leah asked. 'I'll show you a different one if you want.'

Mark stood up and walked towards the computer desk. As he moved he faded, his edges blurring, but once he was sitting at the desk, he seemed more solid again. Leah looked back at her bed. There was no dent where he'd been lying, not even in the pillow.

They played for a while without talking. They were close together, and Leah realised she was occasionally nudging him or would have been – if there'd been anything there to nudge. Her arm and shoulder occasionally crossed with his and she felt nothing. She could put her arm right through him if she chose. It was weird – well-weird.

At the end of a game, Mark turned to her and asked, 'Have you been on Concorde? I expect all planes are Concordes now. You must be able to get to places so fast. I expect you've been all over the world.'

'No, I haven't,' Leah told him. 'And Concorde doesn't fly any more.'

'*What?* You mean there's something better, right? Something even faster?'

'No – I think there was an accident when a Concorde crashed and lots of people died. I'm not sure – and I think they cost too much to run. They weren't making new ones, anyway, and the old ones were getting too old.'

Mark shook his head, sadly. 'I can't believe it.'

'There's a new plane – a really big double-decker one that can take more than 500 people. It's called an Airbus A380 but it's no faster than an ordinary plane and there's not many of them.'

'A *double-decker plane*! Wow! Have you been on one?' Mark asked.

'No – but I can find a picture on the internet if you like.'

'Thanks. I'd like that.'

Leah turned off the game and clicked Internet Explorer. She found websites about the Airbus A380. Mark was thrilled.

'I could print this stuff out – for you to take with you,' Leah began, but she stopped uncertainly. For a moment, she'd completely forgotten he was a ghost.

Mark was shaking his head. 'I can't take anything – there are no things in my world – no bits of paper, no computers, no CDs.'

'I can't imagine it,' said Leah. 'Is there no music?'

'Only in my mind. I've got lots of music there. I like coming here – seeing all your things. I can make things move here and I know it looks like I'm using my hands – but actually, I don't have any real sensation – so I can't feel what things feel like – if you know what I mean. I miss that.'

'I don't understand. How are you so good at computer games?' Leah asked. 'If you can't even feel the joystick...'

'I don't know. I suppose it must be quicker; I don't have to make my muscles move or anything. My hand can respond as quick as my mind – there's no delay. That's what I reckon, anyway.'

'It's incredible,' said Leah.

'Thanks for showing me all that stuff,' said Mark. 'I'll remember most of it – I'll keep the pictures in my mind. That internet is fantastic – it's like having the whole *Encyclopaedia Britannica* in your bedroom only you don't need all the shelves. I'm going to go now.'

'I'm glad you came back,' said Leah. 'You will come again, won't you?'

'Yes – don't worry, I'll be back. 'Bye.'

*

It was the first time he'd actually said goodbye – and hadn't just disappeared without warning. Leah reckoned she must be getting somewhere – he must be starting to trust her more. She thought she preferred him coming earlier, even though there was more chance of her parents coming in. Now it was only eleven and she could go to sleep. For once, she slept surprisingly well.

She had arranged to go round to Nikki's the next evening, when Nikki's dad would be free.

'Hello, Leah,' he said, smiling, as Nikki led her into the lounge. 'I hear you're living in my old friend Mark's house!'

'Yes,' said Leah. She joined Nikki on the comfy sofa, facing her dad who was in an armchair. 'I couldn't believe it when Nikki said you were Mark's friend. The builders found a couple of things that belonged to him and it got me interested.'

'I've had a dig around myself,' said Mark's dad, reaching out for something on the coffee table. 'Look – I found this photo of Mark and me when we were kids.'

He glanced at it, smiling, and had begun to hold it out towards Leah, when Jess burst into the room. She was wearing pink pyjamas and rushed over to Leah, jumping onto her lap, beaming.

'Hi there, Jess,' said Leah, giving her a hug. She felt warm and smelled of bubble bath.

'Will you read me a bedtime story, Leah?' Jess asked. When Leah hesitated she added, 'Please, please, please!'

'I'm talking to your dad and Nikki at the moment,' said Leah. 'How about you go to bed and I'll come up in five minutes and say goodnight.'

'And read me a story?' asked Jess.

'Come on, Jess,' said Nikki, sighing. 'I'll read you a story, while Dad talks to Leah.'

Nikki held out her hand and Jess took it reluctantly, looking back at Leah as Nikki led her out of the room.

'Here,' said Nikki's dad, holding out the photo, now that they were finally in peace.

Leah took it – and had to bite her tongue to stop herself from saying, 'Yes, that's him.' The picture showed two boys aged about nine or ten in shorts and T-shirts. They looked like they were playing in a garden. Mark's thick dark hair and the shape of his face made him easily identifiable. The other boy's hair was also brown but mousier and he had a much rounder face.

'Which do you think is me?' asked Nikki's dad.

'That one,' said Leah. It was easy, when you knew – but she wouldn't have had a clue otherwise. Nikki's dad had a thinner face and a big bald patch now.

He looked pleased. 'Haven't changed much, have I?'

Leah smiled. 'Just a little. How old were you here?'

'I think the year's on the back.'

Leah turned over the picture and read the words

aloud. *'Simon and Mark, August 1976.'*

'1976? It was a real scorcher, that summer – one of the hottest on record.'

'So when did Mark move away?' Leah asked.

'Must have been 1979 or thereabouts,' said Nikki's dad. 'We were in the second year of secondary school – the same school you and Nikki go to.'

'Really? Nikki didn't say you went to our school. So where did he move to?'

'Scotland, I believe.'

'Why Scotland?' Leah asked.

'I think his mum had a relative there or something.'

'Nikki said you lost touch – but did you stay in contact for a while after he moved?'

'He said he'd write but he never did,' Nikki's dad explained. 'He hadn't even left me his new address. I remember being quite upset about it at the time. My mum said maybe he wanted to make a clean break of it and that he was probably busy settling into his new life.'

'What do you mean, clean break?' Leah asked.

'He had some trouble with . . .'

'Leah! Why haven't you come?' called Jess, bursting into the room. 'I've been waiting and waiting and waiting and . . .'

'Jess!' said Nikki, grabbing her in a hug from behind. 'I told you to stay in bed and I'd come and get Leah. Go back upstairs!'

'I'm coming right now,' said Leah, sighing.

She put the photo down on the table and stood up. 'Will you still be here when I come down?' she asked Nikki's dad. 'There's more I'd like to ask.'

Nikki's dad smiled, nodding. 'If you manage to escape from the clutches of our Jess before midnight, then yes, I'll be here.'

Eleven

As soon as Leah reached Jess's room, Nikki said, 'Right, I'll leave you to it,' and disappeared into her own room.

Jess jumped into bed, grabbing the cuddly monkey Leah had given her for her birthday and hugging him close. Leah was pleased to see she had chosen well.

Jess pointed to a pile of books on the bedside table, before sliding under the covers, only her face peeping out.

'Nikki's already read to you, hasn't she?' said Leah.

'Only one book,' said Jess. 'You can read me the rest.'

'What – all these?' Leah exclaimed.

'Yes.'

'No – if Nikki read one, then I'll read one,' said Leah. 'That'll be fair, won't it?' She didn't wait for an answer. 'Which one do you want?'

Jess handed Leah a book called *The Rainbow Pony*. Leah sat beside her on the bed. She'd never read a bedside story like this before. For a moment, she felt self-conscious, reading aloud, but she soon forgot herself.

'You're a good reader,' said Jess, when she came to the last page.

'Thank you,' said Leah. She was sure Jess was about to demand another book but to her surprise, Jess yawned and closed her eyes.

'Night night, sleep tight,' Leah said softly. It was what her mum had always said to her when she was little.

Leah crept out of the room, and met Nikki in the hallway.

'She's not asleep?' Nikki asked in disbelief.

'Shhh,' said Leah, nodding, and putting her finger to her lips.

Nikki raised her eyebrows. 'You're a miracle worker. D'you want to come and put her to bed every night?'

'It was just beginner's luck, I expect,' said Leah, as they went downstairs.

'So what else did you want to ask me?' said Nikki's dad, back in the lounge. 'I don't think there's much more I can tell you. Did you want to know what your house looked like back then? I'm not sure I can remember – I didn't go there much. Mark preferred to come to my place.'

'Why was that?' Leah asked.

'Oh – more relaxed atmosphere, I guess. His dad could be a bit strict.'

'You said Mark didn't write after he moved away,'

Leah reminded him. 'You said something about a "clean break". What did he need a clean break from? I mean, had something happened?'

'His parents hadn't been getting on, that's all,' said Nikki's dad. 'He never said much about it to me but I could tell things were difficult. When he said he and his mum were going to move away he sounded so pleased. I remember being upset – I mean, we'd been friends for years – even though we weren't as close at secondary school. I'd have expected him to at least be a little bit sad that we wouldn't see each other any more.'

'But he wasn't?' Leah asked.

'It didn't seem like it – but then he said it was a secret about moving – and I was the only one he'd told. He made me promise not to tell anyone else. So I felt better – knowing I was the one he'd chosen to tell, and that he trusted me.'

'But why was it a secret?' Leah asked.

Nikki's dad frowned. 'I never thought about it. I guess – maybe because he was ashamed about his parents splitting. It was rare in those days. I think there was only one other boy in our year with divorced parents and he was a bit off the rails.'

'You said Mark's dad was strict – do you remember much about him?' Leah asked.

'His dad? Why do you ask that?'

'I . . . I'm just trying to build up a picture of life in my house when they were living there,' said Leah.

'I told you about that *Top of the Pops* cassette, Dad, remember?' said Nikki. 'Mark's dad sounded horrible.'

'He was a large man – I was always a bit scared of him,' said Nikki's dad, 'though he was friendly enough to me.'

'Did he used to hit Mark?' Leah asked.

'Hit him? I don't know about that – maybe. Mark used to bruise easily – he was always in the wars. I'm sure that was just from playing about – but I think his dad was a bit of a disciplinarian. It was more acceptable to smack kids back then. Mark certainly used to get sent to bed with no supper for the slightest thing. He told me that once – he'd accidentally spilt a drink on the table and had been sent straight to bed. I thought that was terribly harsh.'

'But he never told you his dad hit him,' Leah repeated.

'No – but I don't think Mark would have said anything – even if he did. It wasn't the kind of thing you talked about. Anyway, what is this? A child protection investigation? It's thirty years too late for that!' Mark's dad stood up, shaking his head.

'Sorry – I'm curious, that's all,' said Leah.

'I'm sure it was for the best that he moved away with his mum. I told Nikki I'd have a look on *Friends Reunited* and see if he's listed but I haven't had a chance yet. It'd be fun to get in touch and see what he's doing now.'

'Thanks,' said Leah.

Back at home, Leah was met by her mum, who looked tired and cross. There was no 'How was your day, Leah?' Instead, her mum said, 'You went out and left your music on. This isn't like you, Leah.'

'Sorry – must have forgotten,' said Leah.

She went up to her room angrily. She knew she'd turned the computer off and her music. What had Mark been doing? Had he been surfing the net while she was out?

She looked to see which CD had been playing. It was one she hadn't listened to for years. She snapped it back in the case and clicked 'Internet Explorer' on the computer. She looked at today's history. She was right. Mark had been looking at sites about the double-decker plane and about space travel and – a website about Utah. Why was he looking at that? The final site was one for a company Leah had never heard of. She clicked on it. The website looked familiar. It was the company Jeff Hystaff worked for, the one where she'd found his email address. Mark must have searched for 'Hystaff' on Google, just as she had done. She'd found that Utah site too when she looked for Hystaff.

Had Mark emailed his uncle? Surely not. Anyway – she hadn't shown him how to email, had she? She checked Hotmail. There was nothing. She breathed a sigh of relief. She'd have had some explaining to do if Jeff Hystaff received an email from Mark that was sent from her email address.

At school the next day, Nikki came hurrying up.

'I got Dad to look last night at *Friends Reunited* but Mark wasn't on there,' she told Leah.

'Never mind,' said Leah.

'But Dad's found quite a few other mates from his year on it and he's contacted them. You've got him thinking about his school days – he's even talking about organising a reunion for their year. And he wants to find Mark somehow – and catch up on old times.'

'Can you imagine us having a reunion for our year when we're forty?' Nikki added, giggling. 'I wonder what everyone will be doing.'

'Ryan Field will be in prison and Hannah Lawson will be a barrister,' said Leah.

'Jenna will have six kids – all by different fathers!' added Nikki. 'That's what I reckon!'

'What about you and me?' asked Leah.

Nikki went quiet for a moment. 'Who knows?'

Leah was quiet now too. Had Mark ever thought about it when he was their age? What had been his hopes?

'I wonder if any of the teachers who taught in the 1970s are still here now,' said Nikki.

'I doubt it,' said Leah. 'It's a long time ago.'

'Maybe Mr Reid. He's pretty ancient, isn't he?' said Nikki. 'Or Mrs Keeble. I'll ask my dad tonight.'

'Look!' said Leah. 'There's Mr Reid. I could ask him how long he's worked here. Mr Reid! Can I ask you something?'

Mr Reid stopped in the corridor and turned round. 'Yes?' he said.

'I was wondering how long you've been teaching here?' asked Leah.

Mr Reid smiled. 'Too long,' he said. 'I'll be retiring this summer.'

'So?' said Leah.

'I started working here in...ooh...1977. It was my second teaching job. I've been here ever since.'

'Wow!' said Leah. 'That's a long time. I can't imagine it.'

Nikki came up and joined them. 'Did you ever teach my dad?' she asked. 'Simon Taylor?'

'Simon Taylor? It doesn't ring a bell – but that doesn't mean I didn't. I've taught so many over the years. To be honest, I only remember the ones who stood out in some way – the gifted ones and the very naughty ones.' He smiled again.

'I don't think my dad was either,' said Nikki, looking disappointed. 'He was here from 1978 until 1983. He wants to organise a reunion of his year group. Would you like to come? Even if you didn't teach him, you must've taught some of them.'

'A reunion, eh? Well, you let me know when it is and I'll think about it.'

Leah shifted from foot to foot. All this chat was fine but what about Mark?

Mr Reid was looking at his watch. 'Must dash,' he said, 'and haven't you two got lessons to go to?'

'But, sir,' said Leah. 'Can I just ask you one more thing? Do you remember a Mark Hystaff? He started here the same year as Simon – 1978, but he moved away in 1979.'

Leah felt her fingers crossing as Mr Reid screwed up his eyes thoughtfully.

'No – sorry,' he said finally – and he was gone.

'Shame,' said Nikki.

'Yeah,' said Leah.

Twelve

At school the next day, Nikki showed Leah that she'd brought in the photo of her dad and Mark as children.

'I thought I'd show this to Mr Reid and Mrs Keeble,' said Nikki. 'I asked Dad last night and he said they both taught him. They might not remember the names but they're more likely to remember the faces, don't you think?'

'Yeah – good idea,' said Leah. 'I'll come with you and find them at break, if you like?'

'OK.'

They found Mr Reid first – but although he thought Mark and Simon looked vaguely familiar from the photo, he couldn't be sure and he certainly couldn't actually remember them.

Mrs Keeble seemed to have a much better memory.

'Did you say "Simon Taylor"?' she asked, holding the photo up to the light. 'That's him, isn't it?'

She held the photo out to Nikki – pointing at Simon.

'Yes, that's him, that's my dad,' said Nikki excitedly. 'You remember him, then?'

'He really enjoyed history, if I remember right. My image of him is of a very enthusiastic boy – always with his hand up – though not always with the right answer!'

'I didn't know he was into history at school,' said Nikki. 'But he's got quite a few books about wars and battleships and that kind of thing.'

'Hmm,' said Mrs Keeble. 'Now I'm not so sure about this other boy. What was his name again?'

'Mark Hystaff,' said Leah.

'He left and moved to Scotland,' Nikki added.

Mrs Keeble shook her head, frowning. 'I'm afraid I don't remember him at all.'

Leah felt a pang of sadness. Not to be remembered seemed worse than anything. But Mark had only been at the school for a short time. 'Does the school still have records from the 1970s?' she asked.

'Yes – some, at least – but they're all archived in the basement.'

'I wondered if they might show what school Mark moved to,' said Leah.

'Yeah – that's a great idea,' said Nikki. 'You see, Miss, my dad's trying to organise a reunion of his year at this school. He wants to find Mark because they were good friends. If we know what place in Scotland he moved to – that might help us track him down.'

'When a child moves school,' said Mrs Keeble, 'we

send the records on to the new school, so there's generally a note made in the register. I don't know if that was the case in the 1970s – or how much from that time was kept. Anyway, Mark may well have moved again since then. Have you tried the internet? I'd have thought that would be your best bet.'

'Yes – we've tried that,' said Leah. 'Is there any chance you could look for us – in the records, Miss? If there was something to give us a clue about where he went, it could really help. He might have stayed in the same place, you never know.'

'Please, Miss,' added Nikki.

'Do you think us teachers have got time on our hands to trawl through the archives on a whim?' asked Mrs Keeble. Her eyebrows were raised but she was smiling.

'We'll work extra hard in history,' Leah said pleadingly.

'Well, I do need to go down there as it happens,' said Mrs Keeble. 'It's the school's centenary next year and I'm putting together a pack – one hundred years of Fairmead School. I don't know what made me say I'd do it. I really don't have the time.'

'Maybe we could help, Miss?' Leah suggested.

Miss Keeble looked them up and down thoughtfully. 'Actually – that's not a bad idea at all. It takes so much time going through the files. If you're sure about helping, you could meet me by these stairs at twelve-thirty.'

Leah looked at Nikki, who nodded. 'We'll be there, Miss.'

'That was a great idea of yours about the records,' said Nikki as they walked out into the playground.

Leah smiled. Now that they had something they were both interested in, Nikki was starting to feel more like a real friend.

'I really want to find Mark now,' Nikki continued. 'Dad would be thrilled. I can imagine his face when I say, "By the way, I've found Mark Hystaff – and he's coming to your reunion," or maybe I could just get Mark to turn up as a complete surprise – and not even tell Dad I'd found him!'

Leah nodded but she felt her smile slip. Was it fair to let Nikki get so excited when Mark was dead?

'Don't get too carried away – you don't even know if we'll find him yet,' Leah reminded her.

'I've got this feeling though,' said Nikki. 'I think we will.'

As they waited by the stairs, as arranged, Mrs Keeble was nowhere to be seen.

'She isn't coming,' said Leah, impatiently, but at that moment she came hurrying along the corridor. She unlocked a door near the stairs – a door Leah had never noticed before – and they followed her through it and down a narrow flight of stairs.

The room they entered smelled musty and was

stuffed with filing cabinets and shelves full of boxes with lids.

'We'll have a quick look for your Mark first,' said Mrs Keeble. 'What was his surname again?'

'Hystaff,' said Leah.

'This corner here is the 1970s. The boxes are labelled with years – what year did Mark move away?'

'1979,' said Leah.

'You're sure about that?'

'Yes,' said Nikki.

Mrs Keeble bent over a low shelf, looking at each box. 'I have to warn you, some years are missing altogether,' she said, 'and some have practically nothing in them. Oh – look – 1979. Here we are. Looks like a good year, too – it's a very full box.'

Leah and Nikki helped Mrs Keeble slide the box off the shelf and pull it out into the middle of the room. Mrs Keeble struggled with the lid but it came off.

The box was stuffed full of files. Mrs Keeble trawled through them and then placed two piles on the floor. 'Here – you two can go through these. What year group would Mark have been in?'

'Year 8,' said Leah.

'That would have been the second year, then,' said Mrs Keeble. 'They started counting from one again at secondary level.'

'Here,' said Leah, 'these are the registers, aren't they?'

'Can you find the second years?' asked Nikki.

Leah found them – four registers, altogether. They took one each. Leah scanned the list of names. It was weird thinking all these people were in their forties now – the ones that were alive, that is.

'Look – I've found him!' said Nikki. 'And my dad was in the same class.'

'What does it say?' said Leah, leaning over her.

'It's your address all right – and he had quite a few days off,' said Nikki. 'Look at the crosses. And his last day was 20 March 1979. There are some crosses after that and then a line's been put through.'

'Looks like the school wasn't told in advance that he was leaving,' said Mrs Keeble. 'Turn the page – is there any note in the margin?'

'Yes – here,' said Nikki. 'But I can't make it out. Can you read it, Miss?'

'It looks like: *Note from father – moved away.* Then it says, *No records requested.* And there's a question mark.'

Leah's heart fluttered. 'Isn't that weird, Miss, that the new school never asked for the records?'

'It's unusual – but you said he moved to Scotland, didn't you? The system is different there. Maybe it wasn't the custom.'

Nikki lifted the registers back into the box. 'What a waste of time,' she moaned. 'I really thought we were going to find something and there's nothing at all. How am I going to track Mark down?'

'If you've tried the internet, I'm not sure what else to

suggest,' said Mrs Keeble. 'Now – look at the time! The bell will be going any minute. We'll have to do my research another day – that's if you're still prepared to help me?'

'Of course, Miss,' said Leah – but as she spoke she saw Nikki raise her eyebrows with a despairing look.

As they walked along the corridor to their form room, Nikki was moaning nonstop. 'How many hours do you think she'll expect us to be stuck down there going through that stuff? I wouldn't mind if it had helped us find Mark but...'

'Listen, I'll do it – you can make an excuse if you like,' Leah offered. 'It was me who offered to help her.'

'It doesn't matter. I want to find Mark though – I'm determined to find him.'

'Maybe you should give up,' said Leah. 'Your dad will have plenty of other old friends at the reunion.'

'Give up? I've only just started looking!' Nikki exclaimed, her voice rising crossly. 'It would be great to find Mark and surprise Dad – don't you think?'

Leah shrugged awkwardly. 'Maybe.'

'And I thought you were going to help!' Nikki sounded angry now. 'It's only because of you that Dad wants to meet up with Mark,' she continued. 'I want to make it happen. Are you with me or not? 'Cos if not you can...'

'Nikki Taylor! What is all this shouting about! Stop it right now.'

It was Mrs Fern, their form tutor.

Nikki glared at Leah and huffed off into the class-room.

Leah felt the pain of Nikki's anger and this only added to the tumult of emotions and thoughts churning round in her head, like milk turning to cheese, solidifying into only one conclusion. Mark had left this school without warning. The register confirmed that. It also confirmed that Mark's father was the one who told the school he'd moved away. And no new school had requested the records. That was more significant than anything else.

Mark had never made it to Scotland – Leah was sure, now. Mark had died at his house. His dad had covered it up. If it was an illness or an accident – why would he have done that? Mark's dad had murdered him. It was a horrendous thought – but it was the only conclusion, wasn't it? But she couldn't prove it; she couldn't even prove that Mark was dead.

Leah felt an overwhelming sense of gloom all after-noon. After school she felt reluctant to go home but now Nikki was in a mood, she couldn't go there. There was no other option unless she wanted to hang about on the streets.

She was surprised to find no one around outside or inside the house. She'd noticed the builders had taken to leaving earlier and earlier – but where was Dad?

'Dad,' she called. There was no answer. She went

upstairs – and found the landing covered in dust and a ladder leaning up into the open loft door.

'Dad!' Leah called. 'Are you up there?'

There was a creak and the thud of footsteps and her dad's feet appeared on the ladder, which wobbled precariously.

'Be careful, Dad,' Leah called. 'That doesn't look safe!'

'Hi, love,' he said. 'Glad you're here – you can hold the ladder steady.'

Leah grabbed the bottom of the ladder. 'What were you doing up there?' she asked.

'I need to put in a new water tank. I just wanted to have a look at the old one.'

'Is there anything else up there?' Leah asked.

'Not much – you won't believe what I did find, though!'

'What?' Leah felt a flutter of panic. What had he found – bones? A skeleton? But Dad had reached the bottom now and she could see he looked too cheerful for something like that.

'Round the pipes behind the old boiler,' he said, 'some sort of primitive insulation I guess – to stop the pipes freezing up . . . '

'What are you on about, Dad?' Leah interrupted impatiently.

'Clothes – bags of old clothes – all stuffed round the pipes.'

Thirteen

'Clothes?' Leah repeated, a shudder tingling down her spine. 'What kind of clothes?'

'I don't know – women's clothes, kid's clothes – all sorts. Who knows how long they've been up there.'

'Can I see?' Leah asked. 'Are they still there?'

'If you really want to – but I warn you, some of them have got damp – they're stinky and disintegrating. Best put out for the dustmen, I reckon. If you change out of your school gear and put something old on, I'll pass them down to you.'

'OK – I won't be a sec.'

Leah changed quickly into old jeans and a jumper. Could the clothes in the loft be Mark's clothes? But Dad had said they were women's and kid's. Why had someone stuffed them behind the boiler? Was it like Dad said – to stop the pipes freezing, or had they been put there to hide them?

Once the bags were down she could smell the musty

dampness of the clothes. There were five bags alto-gether. Her dad stood and watched as she knelt down and opened the first one eagerly.

The first thing she pulled out was a dress – a very crumpled, long blue dress covered in yellow flowers. There was a lot of it – she pulled and it seemed to keep coming out for ages. She felt like a magician making strings of scarves appear from nowhere. Finally released, the light fabric billowed as it took over the landing, delighted to have space to expand. It seemed almost alive. Leah flinched as she tried to push it to one side, out of the way.

'Some dress!' said her dad. He took hold of the top and held it up against himself, posing and pretending to dance.

'I don't think it's quite you,' said Leah. She laughed and was glad her dad was there. It struck her that for that moment he was being like his old self – acting the fool, trying to be funny. She couldn't remember when he'd last done that.

She rummaged deep into the bag. Everything seemed to be women's. She pushed the bag aside, reaching into the second bag. She pulled out a pair of jeans. They were flares. She stood up, holding them against her. They were just the right length and although they smelled musty, the fabric was in good condition. They were faded down the front and looked well worn.

'Real 1970s flares, those!' said Dad. 'The original

thing! Must have belonged to someone your age.'

They were Mark's. Leah knew it – she was sure. Her heart beat faster as she pulled out more trousers, T-shirts, shirts, and pairs of shorts. She left them piled on the floor, and moved on to the next bag.

This contained socks and vests and pants. Leah pulled out a few, screwing up her face, and then put them back quickly. She didn't want to touch someone's underwear – *Mark's* underwear. She reached cautiously into the next bag. These things were damp and stank. There were T-shirts, some plain and some tie-dyed, and flowery blouses. Underneath them she found bras and knickers. She dropped them back in and rubbed her hands.

'I think that's enough,' said Dad. 'Let's put them back in the bags and I'll get rid of them.'

'One sec,' said Leah. Something had caught her eye at the top of the remaining bag. She pulled at it. It was a navy blazer – definitely a school blazer. She held it up.

'Look – that's your school badge, isn't it?' said Dad. 'Just think – the boy who wore that must have gone to your school.'

Leah examined it, looking inside the collar. There was a name label, sewn in – '*Mark Hystaff*'. She stared at it. She'd known – she'd been sure – but now there was no doubt, no doubt at all.

'Name label, is it?' said Dad.

'Mark Hystaff,' said Leah quietly. 'It was his maths

book that I found, remember? Dad...isn't it a weird thing to do,' she added, thinking aloud, 'to stuff all these clothes in bags behind the boiler? Why didn't they give them to charity shops or something?'

'There weren't so many charity shops back then,' said Dad, 'but there were jumble sales – plenty of those. Who knows? Perhaps they couldn't be bothered – or they were more concerned about the pipes freezing up.'

Leah put the blazer down and knelt on the floor, reaching further into the bag. There was something hard at the bottom. What was it? She pulled. It was a shoe – a black school shoe – and here was the other.

'You wouldn't use shoes for the pipes,' she said, 'would you, Dad?'

Dad shrugged.

Leah had felt mesmerised by the clothes. She'd been pulling them out of the bags without thinking anything. But now she had stopped and she felt her hands shaking as she stared at the shoes – *Mark's shoes.*

'What's the matter?' Dad asked.

Leah breathed in deeply and out again.

'What is it?' said Dad.

She opened her mouth but the words wouldn't come.

'Leah – are you all right?'

'I think...' she said finally, still staring at the shoes, 'I think Mark's dad murdered him.'

'You what?' said Dad.

'I think he murdered him – and his mum too, because they were going to leave and he didn't want them to go – and he hid their clothes up in the loft – behind the pipes where no one would find them.'

Her dad's eyes had widened as she spoke. 'Leah – what's got into you? What on earth makes you think something like that?'

Leah was shaking all over now – not just her hands.

'Let's go downstairs, get cleaned up and have a drink,' said her dad. He reached down to touch her shoulder. She let him help her up and leaving the clothes and bags, she followed him downstairs.

'Feeling better?' Dad asked, a few minutes later, when they were sitting side by side on the sofa with mugs of tea.

Leah leaned against him, glad for the warmth and comfort of him so close. It was a long time since she'd felt any comfort from him. He'd been so distant. She wished she could enjoy it – she wished she didn't have to think about Mark.

'What were you saying upstairs?' Dad asked.

Leah tried to explain.

'One sec,' said Dad. 'Are you saying your friend Nikki's dad was friends with the boy who lived in this house?'

'Keep up, Dad,' said Leah, impatiently. 'Listen, I'll say it again.'

'A bit more slowly,' said her dad.

Leah began again.

'So?' said Dad, when she'd finished.

'So – Mark's dad must have found out they were planning to leave and killed them. Then he hid their clothes up in the loft so he could pretend they'd moved away. It must be what happened. Don't you see, Dad?' She clutched his arm.

'Leah! Leah! I think you're getting carried away,' said Dad. He put his mug down on the side table and patted her hand. 'Let me think this through. Now – if Mark and his mum left like Simon said, they probably didn't take all their clothes with them, did they? Just what they could carry – right? Especially *if* Mark's dad had a history of violence – and that's a big if from the sound of it! But *if* they left for that reason, then Mark's dad probably shoved their clothes up into the loft, and thought while he was at it, he might as well stuff the bags behind the pipes for insulation. Now doesn't that make more sense?'

Leah sniffed. 'Yes.' The way Dad said it – it did make sense. She wanted to believe every word. But she knew Mark had died. That was the difference.

'I don't know what got you started thinking about murder,' Dad said, shaking his head and hugging her tight. 'You do have some strange ideas, Leah.'

'But Mark's disappeared,' said Leah. 'Nikki's dad is trying to organise a reunion for people from his year at school and he can't find any trace of Mark.'

'People move all over the place these days,' said Dad.

'He could be living in Australia or America or anywhere. Maybe his mum remarried and he took her new name. If that was the case he could be living round the corner and you wouldn't know. There are lots of reasons why he might *seem* to have disappeared.'

'But Dad...'

'I wouldn't worry about it, love. I'm sure he's somewhere.'

He is, thought Leah. He's a ghost. He's here sometimes – upstairs, in my room. But she couldn't say that to Dad, could she? For a brief moment she thought about trying – or at least asking Dad if he believed in ghosts. But he was looking at his watch.

'Your mum will be home soon. I'd better deal with that stuff we left all over the landing.'

'I'll help you,' said Leah.

'No, no – you stay here and relax. You're OK now?'

'Yes – I'm sorry – I shouldn't have gone on like that.'

'Try to think about nice things,' said Dad. 'That helps me sometimes – like how lovely this house is going to look when I've finished it.'

Leah managed a half-hearted smile. 'You're OK too, Dad, aren't you?' she said. 'You're getting better.'

Dad nodded. 'I'm on the mend,' he said. 'It's you I'm worried about now.'

Leah felt a twinge of guilt. What had Mum kept saying – about not worrying Dad, not upsetting him? Just when he was starting to act human again, she was trying to turn everything upside down – talking about murder having happened in this house. It was lucky he didn't believe her – it might have set him right back. Mum would go mad if she knew.

'Don't say anything to Mum, will you?' she asked. 'I'm fine, honest, Dad.'

Mark
Blackout

I am seven years old and something has changed in my house. Dad is happy. I haven't seen his monster face for days. It's like a magician has waved a magic wand and changed him into someone else. I don't know why – and I won't ask – in case it breaks the magic spell and everything goes back to normal.

I sit watching telly with him and he doesn't even yell at me to stop fidgeting. Then Mum comes in and I can't believe my eyes. She's wearing a long blue dress with flowers on it – a lovely dress. I've never seen Mum in a dress this pretty. But it's not just the dress – it's Mum. Someone's done magic on her too. She's got the biggest smile I've ever seen – she is beaming – it really looks as if light is shining out of her face. She twirls in the dress and the flowers swirl round her legs. She looks beautiful.

'So? What do you think?' she asks.

Dad whistles in appreciation.

'You look like a beautiful princess,' I tell her.

'Your dad and I are going out tonight,' Mum tells me. 'It's our anniversary. Kathy is coming round to baby-sit. You'll be a good boy, won't you?'

'Can't I come with you?' I ask. Mum and Dad never usually go out in the evenings. Dad goes to the pub on his own but never both of them. I don't want a baby-sitter — especially not Kathy. She lives down the road and she's got massive teeth.

'No, pet,' says Mum. 'It's just me and Dad tonight.'

I want to protest but they both look so happy, I can't help being happy too — even if I can't go with them and I have to put up with Kathy.

After Mum and Dad have gone, Kathy and I argue about the telly. I want to watch Dr Who but Kathy isn't interested and she says it'll scare me. I beg and plead and in the end she says I can watch it but only if I go to bed early. It's so exciting I bounce up and down on the settee but then the Cybermen appear and it starts getting really creepy. I don't want Kathy to know I'm scared or she might turn it off so I sit biting my nails. That's when the lights go out, the telly goes off and everything's suddenly dark and quiet.

It's a power cut. I know because we've had them before. They keep happening. It's because of the miners' strike. The street-lights are off outside and everything.

'No! No!' I cry. 'Not now — how will we ever know what happened? Do you think the Cybermen got them?'

'I expect the Doctor saved the world in the end,' said Kathy. 'Flipping miners. Who do they think they are?'

116

'When'll it come back on?' I ask. I don't like the dark. I wish Mum was here.

'Who knows?' says Kathy. 'Where does your mum keep the candles?'

'I don't know.'

'You must know!'

'I don't.'

'Great. I knew I never should have said I'd baby-sit. At least I know where the flipping candles are in my place. Haven't you got a torch or something?'

'I've got one upstairs,' I tell her. 'But the battery's run out. What are we going to do?'

'You'd better go to bed,' she tells me.

'But I can't,' I protest. 'It's too early and anyway I might fall down the stairs and what happens if I need to pee? I'll have to come down again in the dark. And I might pee and miss the toilet.'

'Shut up, Mark,' says Kathy. 'Just go to bed and stop making such a fuss.'

'But I can't...'

'Yes, you can. You can feel your way.'

'But...'

I can't tell Kathy but really I'm scared of the Cybermen. That shape in the corner looks just like one.

'Will you come with me, Kathy?'

'Flipping hell. Come on then.' She grabs my arm and pulls me roughly to my feet. 'You go in front – you know your way round this house better than me. Ouch!'

117

She lurches, wrenching my arm. 'What's the matter?' I say, panicky. 'Is it a Cyberman?' I regret my words instantly.

She leans down, clutching her foot and then feels around on the floor. 'A Cyberman? I just trod on a sodding Lego brick, that's all.'

A Lego brick. Things must have changed in this house. Dad would never have let me get away with a Lego brick on the floor. He'd have spotted it straight off and I'd have been in big trouble. That's how much he's changed. He didn't even notice it.

All the same – I'd better not leave it there.

'Where is it?' I ask Kathy.

'Where's what?'

'The Lego brick.'

'I dunno – I kicked it under the settee,' says Kathy. 'Never mind that. Come on. What are you doing?'

I'm crouching down, feeling under the settee. I've got it. I clutch it tight, so tight I hurt my hand. Kathy pulls me up. I feel giddy with the darkness. I'm sure that's a Dalek in the hallway.

I try to stop myself but I start to whimper. 'I hate this. I hate this.'

'You can quit that whining. I'm not having a bundle of laughs meself,' says Kathy. 'Where's the bleedin' stairs?'

'Here,' I say, reaching forward and feeling to check. I clutch the banisters and feel my way up, with Kathy close behind. I hurry past the airing cupboard door in case a Cyberman bursts out.

I am relieved to find my bedroom and feel my way to my bed but then a new fear comes. 'You won't leave me up here in the dark, will you, Kathy?'

'What are you? A little scaredy-cat? I knew you shouldn't be watching Dr Who.'

'It's pitch dark. I don't want to be on my own. Please!'

At that moment the front door bangs.

'There you go – you won't be on your own now,' says Kathy. 'They must've come back early 'cause of the power going off. See-ya!'

'Kathy!' I protest – but she's fumbling her way down the stairs.

I start to follow but it's too dark. I can't see a thing. I turn back and clamber onto my bed, still fully dressed. I cling to my pillow, still clutching the Lego brick. I am reassured by Mum's voice. I can hear her talking to Kathy and Kathy answering. Then the door bangs again. There's silence. For a moment I think they've all gone – and left me here alone – in the pitch dark.

'Mum!' I call. 'Mum!'

'Coming, pet!' she calls. 'Won't be a sec – I'll just fetch a candle.'

Soon I hear her on the stairs and she appears with a lit candle on a saucer. It lights her face but it isn't the beaming beautiful face I saw earlier. It's more like her old face.

'Where's Dad?' I ask.

'He's just walking Kathy home. It's not very nice out there in the dark.'

'It wasn't nice in here neither,' I say.

'You're all right, though?' She touches my face. 'Let's get you into your pyjamas.'

'Were you scared, Mum, when the power went off?' I ask her.

'Not scared exactly but it wasn't too pleasant. We were in a restaurant. We'd only had the first course. It was chaos – no one could see what they were eating. Waiters were holding plates of food and didn't know where to put them down. And of course the kitchen was in chaos too – with half-cooked food and all the cookers and ovens off.'

'So you came home?' I ask.

'We all waited a bit for it to come back on but when it didn't, people wanted to leave and they were all tripping over the chairs and each other and no one could find their coats. Then when we did get out and find the car, the traffic lights weren't working and we got stuck on the road for ages. We were supposed to be having a lovely meal and then going dancing. What a disaster. Why tonight, of all nights?' Mum sighs, shaking her head.

I'm tucked up in bed when Dad gets back. Mum has left the candle by my bed and told me to be careful not to knock it over. She'll come and blow it out once I'm asleep.

Dad thumps up the stairs. I wonder if he'll come and say goodnight but he doesn't. Soon I hear Mum and Dad in their bedroom. Dad is yelling at Mum and she's crying. I wonder why he's angry. The power cut wasn't Mum's fault. I know what's going to happen but I don't want to hear. I bury my head under the pillow to block out the sound.

The magic spell has been broken. The power cut must have done it, that's what. I hate the miners. It's all their fault.

FourTeen

Leah didn't want to go to bed that night. She knew she wouldn't sleep. She couldn't bear to be in her room and she couldn't stop thinking about the clothes. But Mum was home and so far Dad had kept his word and said nothing to her. Leah knew she couldn't start making a fuss. And what was the alternative? Where else could she sleep?

She lay, tossing and turning until a voice interrupted.

'What's the matter?'

Leah's head whacked the headboard. Mark was sitting on the end of the bed. He hadn't been there a second ago and now he was.

'You're the matter, that's what,' Leah said sharply, rubbing her head.

Mark looked surprised. 'Me? Why? What have I done? Do you want me to go?'

'No – no, don't go,' said Leah. She didn't want him here – but she didn't want him to go either.

'Tell me what's wrong then,' said Mark.

Leah hesitated. How would Mark react if she mentioned the clothes?

'If I tell you, then you *will* go,' she said. 'It's about you and what happened to you. Anytime I mention it you disappear, so there's no point, is there?'

'I didn't come here to rake over the past,' said Mark. 'I came because I wanted to know about the future – I mean – I want to know about now, the future I never had.'

'Couldn't we make a deal?' Leah suggested. 'You tell me what I want to know about the past and then I'll tell you anything you want to know about life now.'

'Maybe,' said Mark, but he didn't look keen.

'I don't want to upset you,' said Leah. 'It's just – this is my home now – and if something happened here in the past I want to know.'

'You don't,' said Mark. 'You think you do but you don't.'

They were both silent for a moment.

'Well, let's make it easier,' said Leah. 'We'll start the other way round. Tell me one thing you want to know – and then I'll ask you something.'

Mark was still silent.

Leah had a moment of inspiration. 'Hang on – I've got an Argos catalogue here somewhere.'

She found it buried under piles of school books and sat beside him on the edge of the bed. 'This'll show you the kind of things you can buy today.'

Mark said nothing but he leaned forward eagerly as she flicked through it.

Leah stopped at microwaves. 'Here – did you have a microwave?'

'What is it?' Mark asked.

'You cook food in it,' Leah told him. 'It cooks really fast – you can do a jacket potato in about six minutes.'

'How does it do that?' Mark asked, but he didn't sound very interested.

'I'm not sure – I think it cooks food from the inside out with waves of energy.'

'So you don't have ovens any more then?'

'Most people have both. We've only got a microwave right now because Dad's knocked down the old kitchen.'

Leah was about to explain how microwaves don't brown food in the same way but Mark was turning the pages.

'Wow! Look at the tellies! They're massive – and are they really flat like that or is it just the picture?'

'Yeah – the plasma screen ones are flat. They're mega expensive though.'

Mark glanced at the price and his eyes boggled. 'How can anyone afford that?'

'Not everyone can,' said Leah, 'though I guess people get paid more now. There's hundreds of channels now too.'

'Hundreds! We had three!'

'I can show you the TV Magazine sometime,' said Leah. 'See if any programmes you knew are being repeated. Maybe you'd like to watch them.'

'Nah,' said Mark. 'I'd rather see the new ones.'

He went quiet, flicking further through the catalogue. Leah began to feel impatient.

'I think it's my turn now,' she said, pushing it closed.

'Go on then, what do you want to know?'

'About your clothes . . .' Leah began.

'*Clothes?*' Mark looked bemused. 'I don't think my clothes are much different from yours. I thought everyone would be wearing all-in-one shiny clothes or something like that by now.'

'I think 1970s style is in fashion again now,' said Leah. 'Anyway – it's not about what you're wearing now. It's about the clothes my dad found in the loft.'

She held her breath, waiting for his reaction.

'In the loft?' he repeated. 'They won't be mine. Must be someone else's – someone who lived here after.'

'They're yours and your mum's,' Leah said firmly. 'The school clothes had your name sewn in.'

'Show me,' said Mark, in disbelief.

Leah wished she'd kept something – just the school blazer, at least. 'My dad's chucked them,' she told him. 'They were rotten and they stank.'

'Must've been from when I was little, then,' said

Mark. 'Mum must have put them up there as keepsakes and forgotten all about them.'

'The jeans were the right length for me,' Leah said, shaking her head. 'They would still fit you now. And there was a long blue dress with flowers on it. It was your mum's, wasn't it?'

His eyes widened. '*That dress?* That was old. Mum only wore it once.'

'Those clothes were put up in the loft after you died,' Leah said crossly. 'They were, weren't they? You and your mum – you both died, didn't you? You both died, here in this house. Tell me that's true.'

Mark was quiet and still.

'Come on – tell me.' Leah wondered if she'd gone too far but there was no going back now.

'You think it's a fair exchange?' Mark said finally. 'You tell me about microwaves and I tell you about...about my past. I thought you'd know what it's like – after what you've been through, I thought you'd understand.'

Leah stared at him indignantly. 'What do you mean, *what I've been through?*'

Mark's eyes met hers and seemed to penetrate deep inside. 'You've been through something bad, haven't you? And not too long ago. You know about hurt and pain and confusion – all that.'

'No, you're wrong,' said Leah, looking away. 'Nothing so bad happened to me. It's my dad that's been through it.'

She felt on edge. Her voice grew squeaky as she continued. 'Anyway, what do *you* know about it?'

'Nothing – except that it's there,' said Mark. 'I can sense it – my senses are much stronger now I'm like this. I can feel that you've been through it – and I can feel that you don't want to talk about it. That's why I haven't asked you to, unlike *you*, interrogating *me*. Go on – why don't you tell me what happened to you? *Then*, maybe I'll tell you about me.'

He folded his arms and looked at her defiantly.

Leah felt her control slide away. She stood up and faced him, arms folded tight. 'Get out of here!' she yelled in fury. 'Just go!' She picked up the Argos catalogue from the bed and threw it at him. Of course, he didn't even flinch as it sailed right through him onto the floor. But she saw the hurt expression on his face before he faded to nothing.

Leah found she was sobbing. She climbed back under the duvet. Surely her parents had heard her shout – or heard the thud of the catalogue. She wished one of them would come and comfort her, make everything OK. But no one came.

She sobbed herself into a sleep full of the most dreadful nightmares. It was like a horror film, a vivid, terrifying concoction of everything bad: what had happened with Dad, what seemed to have happened to Mark and the worst of her imagination to complete the package.

She woke sobbing once again. She wished Mark's

ghost had never appeared. Then she wouldn't have to know about him – and she wouldn't need to know what had happened in this house. And as to her own stuff – what business was that of Mark's? It hadn't happened here. It didn't belong here – and it hadn't affected her, no matter what she'd seen. He had no right to ask her about it.

'What's the matter?'

Leah sat up with a start. But it wasn't Mark's voice this time. It was Mum.

'You should be up by now. I'm running late.'

Then Mum saw her face and her tone changed. 'Are you all right, Leah? Look at you – your face is all red. Have you been crying? You *are* crying!'

'It's nothing,' Leah said, trying to wipe the tears away.

'It doesn't look like nothing to me,' said Mum. She sat down on the bed.

'You'd better go – I don't want you to be late,' Leah snuffled.

'I can't go and leave you like this. Dry your eyes and talk to me.'

'I'm just being silly – I've got no reason to cry, not really,' Leah said.

'We've been through a hard time, all of us,' said Mum. 'I know it hasn't been easy for you – and it's no fun living on a building site.' She paused. 'Do you know what I think?'

'What?'

127

'I think you could do with a holiday – a break from all this.'

'Yeah right,' said Leah, sarcastically.

'No – I mean it. You've got half term in a couple of weeks, haven't you? Give me a chance and I'll have a think – see if we can organise something. It won't be anywhere exotic – but I think a break would really do you good.'

Leah visualised herself lying on a sun lounger by a hotel pool in Spain. Yes, she thought. That would do me good. But they couldn't afford even that, could they?

Fifteen

There would be no sun loungers round the pool.

'I've called my friend Kate – you remember her?' Mum had said.

Leah nodded. She vaguely remembered Kate as an old university friend of Mum's whom she had met a few times years ago. Kate was a bubbly, cheerful woman and Leah had liked her.

'She's invited us to stay with her for half term,' Mum continued.

'You mean, you asked her if we could stay,' Leah corrected.

'No – she offered,' Mum insisted. 'She has a lovely cottage in a village and it's only about two hours' drive from here. It's not the most exciting place in the world but it'll be a nice break.'

'It'd be you and me?' Leah asked.

'Yes,' said Mum.

'What about Dad?'

'He's much better at the moment – and he agrees that you need a break – and me too. He wants us to go.'

'Doesn't *he* need a break?' Leah asked.

'He says he'll be able to get on much faster without us here. He reckons he'll have that wall up by the time we get back. And we'll speak on the phone every day.'

So now she and Mum were in the car, on the way to Rivershall, where Kate lived. Leah had been disappointed at first but now she was just glad to get away – glad to go anywhere. The thought of sleeping in a house that wasn't haunted was enough.

'Not far now,' said Mum. 'I hope it's not going to rain.' The sky was ominous, heavy with dark clouds. 'Can you check the directions? Where do we need to turn off?'

Leah grabbed the piece of paper on which Mum had scribbled Kate's directions. 'It's the A204,' she told Mum. 'You go right at the next roundabout, then you take the third turning on the left and that's Freestyle Road.'

'One step at a time,' Mum complained. 'What's first?'

'The A204 at the roundabout – look here it is, coming up.'

As they reached the roundabout Leah looked at the road signs. The road on the left was signed 'Leaverton, 1 mile'.

'Leaverton?' Leah said aloud, thoughtfully. There was something familiar about that name.

'Leaverton – that's left!' said Mum, confused. 'I thought you said right.'

'Yes – go right!' said Leah, as Mum swerved the car.

'What were you on about Leaverton for when we needed to go the other way?' Mum said crossly. 'You nearly made us have an accident.'

'Sorry,' said Leah. 'The place name – it sounded familiar, that's all.'

'Leaverton? Well, you haven't been there, not as far as I know,' said Mum.

Suddenly it clicked. The email from Jeff – Leaverton was where Mark's dad now lived. And it was only a mile from where she'd be staying. Leah's heart sank. It was impossible to get away – she'd travelled for two and a half hours and it was as if Mark was still with her.

'God, Leah, you look frightful.'

These were Kate's words of greeting. She hugged Leah's mum. 'What have you been doing to the poor girl?'

'She's a bit under the weather, that's all,' said Mum. 'It's good of you to have us – I'm sure the break will do us both good.'

'You know you're always welcome,' said Kate. 'It's been ages. Come on in. Let me take that bag.'

The cottage was pretty and cosy and Leah liked it immediately. Kate bustled around, showing them the chintzy rooms and making them feel at home.

'It's so quiet here,' Leah commented, as they sat down with drinks at the kitchen table.

'Yes, too quiet sometimes,' said Kate.

'No man in your life then?' Mum asked, smiling.

Kate laughed and rolled her eyes.

At that moment two cats came charging through the cat flap, one right behind the other. They began to sniff around Leah and Mum's legs.

Leah bent down to stroke the nearest one, which was pale ginger. 'Aren't you soft?' she commented.

The cat came closer, enjoying the attention and then surprised Leah by jumping onto her lap.

'Ooh – he likes you!' said Kate. 'He's called Sandy. The tortoiseshell one is Pebbles. I hope you're OK with cats – not allergic or anything? I didn't think to ask.'

'No, I'd love a cat,' said Leah, wistfully.

'Maybe when the house is finished,' said Mum.

Kate was vegetarian and had cooked them a vegetable casserole for dinner. This worried Leah at first, as she was not much of a vegetable eater but to her surprise it was delicious and didn't taste of vegetables at all. After the meal, they went into the comfy lounge and Leah found both cats competing for her lap. She sat, snuggled up amidst their warmth and softness while the rain poured down outside and Kate told them hilarious stories about her attempts at internet dating. It was a long time since Leah had heard her mum laugh so much.

Leah was glad they'd come – and she was sure she would sleep well in Kate's spare room. Mum was to sleep on the sofa bed downstairs.

It was too much to hope for. Leah slept quickly but woke shaking and sobbing. It was the same horrendous nightmare. She didn't realise she must have actually cried out, until Kate came in.

'What is it, Leah? What's wrong?'

Kate was wearing a Winnie the Pooh nightshirt that made her look like an oversized child. She sat down on the bed, and put her arm round Leah, hugging her tight in a way Mum never did. This made Leah sob more.

'Come on, that's right, let it all out,' said Kate.

It was strange to be encouraged to cry. If she was crying Mum always wanted her to stop – even when she was little.

With that thought, Leah found her tears drying up. 'I just had a bad dream,' she told Kate. 'I'm OK now. I was stupid to think I'd be safe here.'

'You are safe here, of course you are,' said Kate.

'No – I meant safe from the nightmare. But it still came.'

'You poor love. Do you want to talk about it?'

Leah was tempted – Kate was so lovely and she wanted to tell her everything. But Kate was Mum's friend. Whatever Leah said, she knew it would get straight back to Mum.

'I thought it was your dad who had the problems,'

said Kate. 'It was terrible – what happened – and after what he did. So unfair! Gilly's been telling me all about him on the phone – but she's never mentioned you being in such a state.'

'Mum works such long hours,' Leah said, defending her. 'And she's had her hands full with Dad. At least he's getting better now. Anyway – I've been OK. I *am* OK.'

Kate shook her head, stroking Leah's hair. 'You don't look OK to me.'

'I'm fine – go back to bed, Kate, really,' Leah insisted.

'If you're sure? But anytime you want to talk – you know I'm here.'

Kate left the bedroom door open and in the morning Leah woke up with a soft, purring cat on each side.

'What would you like to do today?' Kate asked Leah over breakfast.

Leah glanced at Mum. From her worried expression, Leah knew Kate had told Mum about the nightmare.

'I don't know. What is there to do?' she asked, without enthusiasm.

'How about a nice country walk?' said Mum. 'It is supposed to stay dry according to the forecast.'

Leah shrugged.

'There's an ice-skating rink near the ring road if you fancy,' said Kate, 'or perhaps you'd rather go shopping?'

'Whatever,' said Leah.

Kate looked from her to Mum and back in frustration. 'It's your holiday.'

'Leah?' said Mum.

'Shops then,' said Leah.

'I'll take you to Leaverton,' said Kate. 'There's a nice shopping centre there.'

Leah felt a thud in her stomach. *Leaverton.* She was going to Leaverton – going to the place where Mark's dad lived. She might pass him in the street without even knowing.

'I'll help Kate clear up,' said Mum. 'You go and get yourself ready.'

Upstairs, Leah paused outside the small room that Kate used as her study. Through the open door she could see Kate's laptop on the desk. It was on. She could hear Mum and Kate busy talking downstairs. With only a moment's hesitation, she was on the internet and searching the phone directory in Leaverton for the name 'Hystaff'. There it was. 'Hystaff C, 121 Green Road, Leaverton.'

It had to be him. Leah stared at it for a moment, repeating the address in her mind. Then she closed the window, put the mouse back as she'd found it and came out onto the landing.

'You ready then?' Mum said, coming up the stairs. She looked her up and down. 'I think you'll need your jacket. It's not too warm out there.'

'I'll get it,' said Leah.

121 Green Road. Why had she looked it up? she asked herself, as she pulled on her jacket. It wasn't as if she was going to go round there and knock on the door, was it? All the same, as Kate drove them into Leaverton, Leah couldn't help watching out eagerly for every road name they passed. As they turned to go into the multi-storey car park, Leah suddenly spotted it – on the left, a little way ahead. *Green Road.* She only caught a glimpse – but she was sure it was Green Road.

She tried to forget it as they walked towards the shops. She didn't want to think about Mark or his dad but it was impossible to put them out of her mind. As they wandered from clothes shop to clothes shop, Leah couldn't focus on these clothes at all. The clothes from the loft kept flashing through her mind.

'Why don't you try this on?' said Kate, holding up a purple jumper that Leah would never have picked out herself. There was a slight note of desperation in Kate's voice. Leah felt guilty. Kate was trying so hard.

'Yeah – thanks. I will,' said Leah. She took the jumper and headed for the changing rooms. To her surprise, it fitted and suited her well. She took it off and looked at the price tag. Her heart sank. Mum would never let her spend that much on a jumper.

'How was it?' Mum asked. Kate was across the aisle, looking at some skirts.

'It's lovely but it's too expensive.' Leah held up the price tag.

Mum frowned. 'If you really like it...' she began.

Kate joined them. 'Any good?' she asked.

'No,' said Leah. 'It didn't fit.' She met Mum's eyes – which looked partly relieved and partly disappointed. 'I'm sure I'll find something else. Could I go off on my own for a bit?'

'It can't be much fun hanging around with us oldies!' Kate giggled.

'Speak for yourself,' said Mum with a half smile. She turned to Leah. 'Are you sure you won't get lost?'

'I've got my mobile,' said Leah, 'and I won't go far.'

'Let's meet in half an hour in the café,' said Kate. 'It's called Coffee Beans and it's two doors down from this shop.'

'Fine,' said Leah.

Leah walked out of the shop and back towards the car park. When they'd left the car they'd come out of the car park a different way that brought them right into the shopping centre. Leah hoped she could find the way back to Green Road. She knew it was pointless but she felt compelled to go there – to see the house where Mark's dad lived. It was almost as if an invisible force was making her go.

There it was – *Green Road*. Leah took a deep breath and began to walk down it. She looked at the house numbers – 1, 3, 5, 7... There was some way to walk but at last she was there – number 121. She stopped. It was an ordinary semidetached house.

Was Chris Hystaff at home? Leah wondered. What was he like? What kind of life was he leading now?

Why had she come here? What was the point? Leah sighed and turned to walk towards the shops. The sound of a door banging made her glance back. Someone had come out of number 121.

SixTeen

It wasn't a man. It wasn't Chris Hystaff. It was a girl – a girl about Leah's age, with long dark hair in a ponytail. The girl hadn't seen her yet and Leah couldn't help staring, frozen to the spot. Questions rushed through her mind. Who was she? What was she doing coming out of Chris Hystaff's house? She was surely too young to be Chris's daughter – or was she? Could she be his granddaughter – or could Chris have moved out recently and new people moved in?

'Are you all right?'

Leah jumped and felt her face flush red. The girl had seen her and was walking towards her down the path, looking curious.

'Yes…no…actually, I'm a bit lost,' said Leah, stumbling for words. 'Can you tell me the way to the shopping centre?'

'I'm going that way – I'll show you if you like,' the girl said, smiling shyly. 'You're not from round here, then?'

'No,' said Leah, as they began to walk along together. 'I'm from Finswood. I'm just here for half term, staying with my mum's friend.'

'Not much of a place for a holiday,' the girl said. 'I'm Jade, by the way.'

'Leah,' said Leah. 'Have you lived here long? I mean – that was your house you just came out of, wasn't it?'

'About five months,' said Jade, nodding. 'It's handy for the shops. They're not bad – but there's not much else to do round here, only the ice rink. I'm going there tomorrow with my sister. Hey...you could come if you like,' she added. 'That is – if you don't have plans with your mum and her friend?'

'Really?' said Leah. 'You wouldn't mind?' She was stunned by the friendliness of this girl she had only just met.

''Course not. It'd be fun.' Jade smiled.

They had reached the shops. Leah explained about meeting Mum and Kate at the Coffee Beans café and Jade showed her the way.

'If you hold on, I'll ask my mum about tomorrow,' said Leah. 'Is that OK?'

'Sure,' said Jade.

Leah found Mum and Kate huddled on a corner table, deep in conversation. Kate had a pile of bags by her feet.

'Hi,' said Leah.

'How are you getting on?' said Kate. 'Did you find anything nice?'

'Yes – actually,' said Leah. 'I found a friend.'

'A friend?' Mum repeated, her eyebrows rising in surprise.

'She lives down the road from here and she's invited me to go ice-skating with her tomorrow. Can I go? Her name's Jade – she's waiting outside.'

Leah pointed and Mum and Kate both looked round towards the window. Leah was embarrassed when Jade saw them but Jade just smiled and waved.

'She looks like a nice girl,' said Mum. 'I don't see why not.'

Ordinarily Leah knew Mum might have hesitated to let her go off with a complete stranger but she sensed Mum's relief that she was finally looking happy about something.

'Thanks, Mum,' she said smiling.

Leah liked Jade – and wished they could just be friends, going ice-skating. She wished there wasn't that lurking awareness that Jade was somehow connected to Chris Hystaff. There were so many questions she wanted to ask. She felt compelled to find out as much as she could – but she also didn't want to make Jade suspicious in any way.

The next day, Kate had offered to drop her at the ice

rink but she turned out to be rather lax about time and they were twenty minutes late. Leah was pleased and relieved to see Jade waiting by the entrance. She was standing with a much smaller girl, about Jess's age, with short mousy hair.

'Sorry I'm late,' said Leah, hurrying up.

'No worries. I thought you weren't coming,' said Jade. 'I'm glad you did. This is my sister Megan.'

'Hi, Megan,' said Leah, but Megan didn't smile. She looked as shy as Jess was confident.

'Say hello,' said Jade, nudging her. But Megan looked at the ground.

'Don't mind her, she's in a mood,' Jade told Leah.

'No, I'm not,' Megan muttered crossly.

'Come on, let's go in,' said Jade, tutting.

Megan seemed to cheer up once they were on the ice and she had clearly been skating before. Leah hadn't been for years and had some embarrassing skids, nearly doing the splits at one point.

'Are you OK?' Jade asked.

'Yes, I'll be fine once I get going,' said Leah.

'Take my arm,' said Jade. They linked arms and went round together. Leah gradually began to feel steadier on the ice. It felt as if they'd been friends for years.

'Do you like living round here?' Leah asked, when they had stopped for a drink at the rink-side café. They were watching Megan, who was still skating.

'It's all right,' said Jade. 'We weren't far away before – just the other side of Leaverton. We were in a flat then – so the house is much nicer. What's it like where you live?'

'It's nothing special – it's a bigger town so there's not as much green everywhere like here. We moved recently and my dad's doing loads of work on the house so it's like a building site at the moment.'

'Crap,' said Jade, sympathetically.

'How come you moved from the flat?' Leah asked.

'My mum was going out with this guy, Chris, and they wanted to live together. He thought our flat was too small so we moved into his place.'

Leah's heart skipped a beat. 'Do you get on with him . . . Chris?' she asked.

'Why do you ask that?' Jade looked at her curiously.

'Oh,' said Leah, thinking quickly. 'I've got a friend with a stepdad and she hates him so I just wondered . . .'

Leah watched Jade's face closely. Was that pain on her face – or was she just thinking?

'The thing about Chris,' Jade said, 'is that people always think he's my granddad. He's heaps older than Mum. It's so embarrassing! I don't know what she sees in him. Oh no! Megan's fallen over!'

Jade leaped up and over the barrier. Leah followed, her heart beating fast as she watched Jade trying to get the bawling Megan to her feet.

'Can I help?' Leah asked, hovering anxiously. 'Do

you think she's badly hurt?'

Megan was crying so loudly that everyone around was staring. Leah held out a hand to help pull her up but Megan pushed it away.

Leah stood back, feeling helpless. With Jess she had felt wanted and useful but Megan was something else.

Jade had finally managed to get Megan to her feet. 'Look – she can stand up all right so nothing's broken,' said Jade. 'Cut the noise, Meg, will you!'

'Should we ask at the desk if there's someone who does first aid,' Leah suggested, 'to have a look at her legs?'

'No – I'll take her to the loos and check but I'm sure she's fine,' said Jade. 'She's just making a fuss over nothing. You wait here – we won't be long.'

'I'll come with you,' said Leah.

'No, there's no need,' Jade said firmly.

Leah sat down at the café and waited. Jade and Megan were living with Chris, their mum's boyfriend who was much older than their mum. It had to be Chris Hystaff – didn't it? It was his name at that address in the phone book, after all. It was hard to take it in. Leah was scared to think about it.

Where were they? They'd been gone ages. Should she go to the toilets and find them? Leah decided to give them one minute more. She thought about Megan and how different she was from Jess. Jess could be a pain but at least she was fun too.

Finally Jade returned, pulling Megan towards the café. She had stopped crying but was still giving little sniffs now and then. She sat down and Jade bought her a milk shake.

'Are you all right now?' Leah asked kindly. 'That was a nasty fall.'

Megan sniffed and ignored her. Leah gave up.

'Kate will be here to pick me up soon,' she told Jade. 'Maybe we can meet up again?'

'Yeah – that'd be cool,' said Jade. 'Sorry about Megan.'

'Don't worry – I've had a good time,' said Leah.

Leah felt shaky that night when she lay in bed thinking about everything. It was hard to believe that Jade and Megan and their mum were living with Mark's dad. Was he violent to them? Were they in danger? Jade had shown no sign of being scared of him – only embarrassed by his age. Could Megan's sullenness be anything to do with him? Or could Chris Hystaff have turned over a new leaf and be living a happy and normal life?

If her theory was right and Chris had killed Mark and his mum, then even if he was behaving OK now – it didn't mean he might not flip and get nasty, did it? Surely Jade and Megan and their mum ought to be warned that they were living with a murderer.

Seventeen

That night Leah slept fitfully, waking what felt like every few minutes, sensing that if she slept any deeper, the nightmares would come. Again she woke, but this time she was sure something had woken her. There was a slight creak, the creak of a door. In the hazy glow of the streetlight through the curtains, she saw that the bedroom door was slowly opening.

She tensed. Had Kate come to check on her? No head appeared round the door. Leah glanced at the bedside clock. It was 3.10 a.m. Her skin prickled as she turned back to the door. It was half open and had stopped moving.

'Kate?' she whispered. Who else could it be?

Someone was there – she could sense it. She reached out for the bedside light switch and had to feel around, her hand shaky as her fingers finally found it.

The light flickered and came on. There was no one there. Leah's eyes told her that but her heart didn't believe it. A ghost? Her heart sank at the thought. Had someone died here too? Now because of Mark, would all ghosts seek her out, knowing she believed?

'Speak to me,' she whispered. 'Go on – I know you're there.'

No one spoke. Leah waited.

She sat still, for what felt like an age. Then she sighed and lay back down, turning off the light. She was stupid, talking into thin air.

There was a sudden thud. Someone had sat down on the bed, close to her legs. Leah let out a scream. She sat bolt upright.

'Leah?'

In an instant the bedroom light was on and Kate was in the doorway, hair standing out in all directions. And on the bed – on the bed – a bundle of ginger fluff. The cat's eyes stared at her curiously.

'Sandy!' Leah mumbled, and she began to sob. 'I . . . I thought . . .'

'Did he give you a fright?' Kate asked. 'I'm so sorry, Leah. You're a rascal, Sandy!' She gave the cat a squeeze. He pulled away and came closer to Leah, nuzzling up to her.

'I think he's saying sorry,' said Kate, sitting down on the bed.

'But how did he get in?' Leah asked, stroking him, and gulping back a sob. 'The door was shut – I know it was.'

'When he's determined enough, he's quite capable

of leaping up and knocking the handle to open a door,' said Kate. 'He likes hiding under beds too.'

Leah began to sob again, not sure why but she couldn't stop.

Kate put a hand on her shoulder. 'Oh Leah, love. Do you want me to get your mum?'

'No, no,' said Leah. 'I'm OK now.'

'I'm so sorry about Sandy,' said Kate. 'I really am.'

'Kate?' Leah began.

'Yes?'

'Do you believe in ghosts?'

Kate laughed and Leah felt herself pull back in embarrassment. Why had she asked?

'I've never seen one myself,' said Kate. 'In my mind, when you're dead, you're dead. That's it and finished. I think I'd prefer it like that, anyway. Why? Did you think Sandy was a ghost, then?'

'No – of course not,' said Leah, instantly on the defensive. 'I just wondered, that's all.'

'Is it to do with your nightmares?' said Kate.

'Yeah.'

'Why don't you tell me about them? It might help to talk.'

'No, it's OK. I'd rather just get some sleep,' said Leah. She'd wanted to talk to Kate. She would have done – if Kate had been open to the idea of ghosts. But she'd laughed. She was never going to understand.

*

'Leah, it's your friend on the phone,' Kate called the next morning.

Leah took the phone eagerly. She'd given Jade Kate's land line as well as her own mobile number as she'd forgotten to bring her charger with her.

'Hi.'

'Hi, Leah,' said Jade. 'I wondered if you want to do something this afternoon?'

'Yeah – that'd be great,' said Leah.

'Do you play tennis?' Jade asked.

'Yes, I love tennis – but I haven't got my racquet with me,' said Leah.

'No worries – I've got an old one you can borrow,' said Jade. 'Can you get someone to drop you at the park gate in Oaktree Road?'

Kate said she and Mum would happily drop Leah there at two. Leah was pleased. If they were going to play tennis at least that meant Megan wouldn't be dragging along. She needed to get Jade alone so that she could talk to her properly.

But as they pulled up at the park later, Leah's heart sank as she saw that Megan had come. How could she talk to Jade with Megan there? How were they even going to get a decent game of tennis?

'Megan wanted to come,' Jade explained, 'but I said only if she would be our ball girl – and you said yes, didn't you, Megan?'

Megan nodded, eyes down, squirming.

'That's great,' said Leah, trying to sound enthusiastic. 'It'll be handy to have a ball girl.'

For the first few games, Megan ran about after the balls but Leah wasn't surprised when she suddenly folded her arms, sat down on the edge of the court and said, 'I'm not doing it any more. I want to go to the swings.'

Jade argued with her – and for a while they carried on playing, ignoring Megan's sulk – but Leah found it hard to concentrate.

'Let's take her to the swings,' she suggested. 'I don't mind, really.'

They walked across the park to the playground. While Megan swung happily back and forth, Jade and Leah sat down on a bench. This is my chance, Leah thought. She had to say something now. She had to find out more about Chris. She had to know if Jade and Megan were in danger.

'Jade ...' she began, unsure quite what she was going to say.

Jade looked up, met Leah's serious eyes and frowned.

'What is it? Is something wrong?'

'I don't know how to ...' Leah began – but as she spoke she felt wet specks on her face and Megan was running over from the swings.

'It's raining, Jade!' she called. 'It's raining!'

'A bit of water won't hurt you,' said Jade. 'It's only a few drops.'

But within seconds it had begun to pour. None of

150

them had umbrellas.

'Jade, I'm getting soaked!' cried Megan. 'It's not fair! You got all that time to play tennis and now it's raining and I got hardly any time on the swings.'

They ran to shelter under a tree, but it didn't give much cover.

'Let's make a run for the house – all right, Meg?' said Jade.

Megan nodded – but glanced at Leah and then questioningly at Jade.

'It's all right,' Jade said quietly to Megan.

What was all right? Leah wondered. But she had no time to ask. The rain was coming down even harder. They ran.

It took about ten minutes to reach Green Road. Leah realised with a jolt that she was about to go into Chris Hystaff's house. As she followed Jade and Megan to the front door, she trod in a puddle and the water splashed up her legs. Chris wouldn't be there, would he? Surely he'd be at work.

Her heart was beating fast as the front door opened. The woman who greeted them was clearly Jade and Megan's mum. She was slim, with Megan's pale eyes and Jade's dark hair. She looked neither as friendly as Jade nor as grouchy as Megan – somewhere in between.

'Look at you!' she said, when she saw the bedraggled bunch of girls. 'Didn't even one of you have an umbrella? Get those shoes off before you come in –

151

there'll be murder if I have muddy footprints all over the floor!'

She spoke jokily but Leah shuddered at the word *murder.* She quickly pulled off her wet shoes and followed Jade and Megan into the hallway. The house was spotless, every surface gleaming almost artificially.

'This is Leah, Mum,' said Jade. 'She came ice-skating with us yesterday.'

'I hope you don't mind me coming back here,' Leah said.

'No, no...that's OK. You'd better get out of those wet things. I'm sure Jade will find you something to put on. I'll leave you to sort yourselves out. I've got to get the dinner on. I'm running behind.'

Leah went with Jade and Megan upstairs to the neat, rather bare bedroom they shared. There was no sign of Chris, to Leah's relief. Jade lent her some dry clothes.

Megan undressed on the floor between the beds but stood up to reach for some dry trousers. As she did, Leah caught a glimpse of the dark bruises on her legs.

'Wow!' said Leah. 'Are those bruises from the ice-skating? They look really bad.'

Megan's eyes narrowed and she crouched down again quickly, struggling to pull on the dry trousers.

Jade intervened. 'You had quite a bump on that ice, didn't you, Meg?'

'Yeah – it hurt,' said Megan, nodding. 'I don't never want to go there again.'

The way Megan had reacted to Leah's question, Leah couldn't help wondering – were the bruises really from ice-skating or, was it possible, could Chris have been hitting her? No – surely not, Leah told herself. After all, she had seen Megan fall.

'How are those jeans?' Jade asked Leah. 'Do they fit?'

'We must be exactly the same size,' Leah said, smiling.

'Come on down and I'll make some drinks,' said Jade.

Megan wanted to stay upstairs and play so Jade led Leah down into the living room and left her there while she went into the kitchen. Leah looked eagerly at the photos on the mantelpiece. There were school pictures of Jade and Megan, and one of their mum with her arms round a tall, stocky man with short greying hair. He was squinting into the sun and smiling. He certainly didn't look like a man who'd murdered his wife and child. Could that really be Chris Hystaff?

'Is that your stepdad?' Leah asked Jade, who had returned with some glasses of orange.

'Yeah. Well – he's not actually my stepdad. He and Mum aren't married.'

'How did your mum meet him?' Leah asked.

'Down the pub,' said Jade.

'Has he got any children?'

'No. Chris never had kids with his first wife. I don't think he's used to being around kids. He's a bit obsessive about tidiness. I think people with kids get used to a bit of mess!'

'What happened to his first wife?' Leah asked.

'They split up years ago,' said Jade, frowning. 'You do ask a lot of questions.'

'Sorry,' said Leah. 'I'm just being nosey – I'll shut up.'

'Your mum was picking you up from the park gate, wasn't she?' said Jade.

Leah nodded.

'You'd better call and get her to pick you up here.'

It sounded like an order to Leah and made her tense slightly. It wasn't the idea itself – Jade was right, she did need to call Mum – but she sensed Jade wanted her to go. Leah looked at her watch. There was only half an hour before she was due to be picked up.

Leah took out her mobile. There was still some power in it, though not much.

'I'll get some biscuits,' said Jade, and disappeared into the kitchen.

Leah walked up and down the room, waiting for Mum to answer. While she spoke to Mum, she glanced at the pile of letters on the side table. The top letter was a window envelope and she couldn't see the name – only the address.

Putting the phone back in her pocket after the call, she lifted the letter, simultaneously shaking it to see the name and glancing at the letter below. Both were addressed to Mr C Hystaff. It was him. She'd had a moment's doubt when Jade said he didn't have kids with his first wife – but that was a lie. It was him. She'd known it – but here was the absolute proof.

'What are you doing?'

Jade's voice made Leah jump guiltily. She dropped the letter and it landed on the pile, tipping several other letters onto the floor. She bent down to pick them up.

'Nothing,' she said, thinking fast. 'I just knocked the letters. I was trying to put them back in the right order so you wouldn't notice. I'm such a clumsy clot – I'm sorry.'

Jade was staring at her suspiciously. 'Is there something you're not telling me?' she asked.

Eighteen

Leah looked away, hiding her face which she could feel was reddening. How could she say anything now – with Jade's mum in the next room and Megan, who might come down any minute? And how would Jade react if she did tell her?

'No...nothing,' she said, sitting down and picking up her drink in as casual a way as she could manage. 'And my mum's on her way.'

Jade held out a plate of biscuits and Leah took a chocolate one.

'Thanks,' she said.

Jade still looked on edge as she put the biscuits down on the table. Leah bit into hers but had to make a big effort to make herself swallow. She was desperate to lighten the atmosphere.

'I can't believe how wet we got!' she said. 'That rain didn't half come down!'

'Yeah,' said Jade.

'Thanks for lending me the clothes,' Leah added.

'That's all right.'

'Is Megan OK? She seems to get upset really easily,' said Leah.

Jade shrugged. 'She's always been like that.'

At that moment the doorbell rang. Leah heard her mum's voice.

'That's my mum. I'd better go,' said Leah, with relief. It felt impossible to make conversation now without sounding like she was prying. 'Thanks for the drink and biscuit.'

As she reached the door, Jade's mum handed Leah a bag with her wet clothes.

'Don't forget these!'

'Thanks,' said Leah. She turned to Jade. 'Maybe we can meet up again before I go back? I'll need to give you back your clothes, anyway.'

'Yeah – I'll give you a call,' said Jade.

But Jade didn't phone – not the next day or the next.

In the end Leah tried phoning herself. 'I wondered if you'd like to meet up,' she asked Jade.

There was a pause before Jade answered. 'Actually – I'm busy today – but thanks for asking.'

'I'm sorry if I—' Leah began but Jade interrupted. Her voice was sharp.

'I told you, I'm busy. Look – I'd better go.'

She had put the phone down before Leah had a

chance to ask what she was busy with – or to arrange to drop off Jade's clothes.

Leah hung about with Mum and Kate, feeling wretched. She'd blown it. She'd clearly made Jade suspicious – though what she suspected Leah couldn't imagine. And she still didn't know much about Chris Hystaff – or if Jade and Megan and their mum were in real danger. If only she hadn't picked up that letter.

'What's up?' Kate asked, her voice sounding unusually serious for Kate. She sat down on the sofa beside Leah, who was curled up with Sandy. Mum was in the bath upstairs.

'I'm fine,' said Leah.

'No – I mean really,' said Kate. 'This is me you're talking to. Have you had any more nightmares?'

'No.'

'It's a shame you couldn't meet up with your friend again,' Kate said.

'She's not a friend, exactly,' Leah found herself saying. 'I mean, we've only known each other a few days.'

'You seemed to be getting on like a house on fire,' said Kate, then she put her hand over her mouth as Leah shuddered. 'Sorry – that's not the best expression, is it? You know what I meant, though?'

Leah said nothing.

'Leah – I know I've said this before – but if there's

something on your mind that you want to talk about, I'm here and now's the time. You're going home tomorrow.'

'I'm OK,' said Leah.

'You're not,' said Kate. 'It's up to you, of course, but I honestly think it would do you good to talk to someone. It seems like there's tons of stuff going round in your head and unless you deal with it...'

'I don't want to talk about it, all right?' Leah said sharply. 'I want to forget it all – that's why we came to stay with you, isn't it? To have a break – get away. Why do you keep wanting me to talk?'

'Because I can see you're brooding,' said Kate. 'And I'm not saying you should talk to me. I wondered – maybe there's a counsellor at your school you could see? It might be easier to talk to someone who's completely unconnected with anyone you know.'

Leah shifted down the sofa, away from Kate, wishing she would shut up. Unsettled, Sandy leapt from her lap onto Kate's.

'We'll go out for a meal for your last night, tonight,' Kate suggested, changing tack. 'There's a nice Italian place in Leaverton – how about that?'

'If you like,' said Leah.

'And we can drop those clothes back into your friend's house on the way,' Kate added. 'I've washed them and ironed them for her.'

*

159

Leah wished she didn't have to go back there. She wanted to forget about Jade and Megan and about Chris Hystaff. She couldn't deal with it – it was too much. Why had they had to come here, near Leaverton? Why had she looked up Chris's address? She wished they could go home now – not home to that creepy building site – but home to their old house, their old life. If only...

As they drove into Leaverton, Leah closed her eyes and imagined just that. It was blissful.

'We're here,' said Kate, as the engine cut, jerking Leah back to reality. 'And if you want a few minutes to say goodbye to your friend, we'll wait. There's no rush. Why don't you get her email address, then you can stay in touch?'

Leah picked up the bag of clothes from the car seat beside her. She tried to stop herself thinking of those other bags of clothes – the ones Dad had found in the loft – but they were already there, in her head. She shuddered as she got out of the car.

She rang the doorbell and waited, wondering if Jade herself would answer it and what she would say. It only occurred to Leah at that moment that it was evening and Chris might be home. What if he...? And then the door opened and he was there.

In shock, Leah felt herself reel back, away from this large man with his short, greying hair. He looked just like his photo, only he was frowning – not in a nasty way, just as if to say, 'Yes, how can I help you?'

She was standing face to face with Chris Hystaff. *Chris Hystaff* – here, right before her eyes.

'You a mate of Jade's?' he asked.

'Y-yess,' said Leah. 'I just came to bring these back. She . . . Jade . . . she lent them to me when we got caught in the rain.'

Chris Hystaff smiled, a warm, friendly smile.

This man couldn't be a murderer – he couldn't, could he?

'Jade's out at the moment,' said Chris. He reached out his hand for the bag. 'I'll make sure she gets it.'

'Thanks.'

The door closed quickly and Leah felt her legs wobbling as she walked back towards the car.

Mark
The Queen's Silver Jubilee

It is 6 June 1977. I am eleven years old. Tomorrow is the Queen's Silver Jubilee. There's going to be a party in my street. We got Jubilee bookmarks at school with silver crowns on them. I wanted a green one but I got red. I don't care really. I showed it to Mum. She said it's lovely – it'll be something to show my grandchildren. Wow!

Mum's making a cake for the party. She should have started it earlier. The kitchen's a mess and Dad will be home soon. I tell her to hurry up. She says I can help wash up but I can't be bothered. It wasn't my idea to make a cake.

I go up to my room and put on some music. I like the Stranglers *and* Bay City Rollers. *Mum calls me to turn it down – Dad'll be home soon. I ignore her but I shut the bedroom door.*

The front door bangs. My stomach lurches. I hate that. I'm pathetic, that's what I am – just like he says. I'm a weed – I need toughening up. Last time he said that I went, 'What, so I can be like you?'

I know I shouldn't have said it. Saying things like that –
it's asking for it, Mum reckons. It just came out, that's all. But
I don't see how beating me to a pulp is supposed to toughen me
up, do you?

I've got the music on and the bedroom door shut but I can
still hear him. Something like, 'And where's my bloody dinner,
then?'

I can see myself in a chef's hat, presenting him with a silver
dish full of blood. That'd be his 'bloody dinner'. It makes me
laugh, but then I think – that dish of blood, it's our blood, isn't
it? It's mine and Mum's. That's what he wants, to drain the
blood out of us.

There's a scream. It's Mum. Something about it makes me
run – down the stairs, towards the kitchen. The door's open.
There's the smell of cake – freshly baked cake – but there's no
cosy family scene to go with it. There's Dad standing there,
with a kitchen knife in his hand, a big, sharp one. Mum's
pressed up against the sink, her face full of terror.

I stop in the doorway. 'Dad! Don't!' I yell.

He turns. I've caught him by surprise. The breath goes out
of me as his eyes meet mine. Why does he hate me? Why? He
swings the knife round towards me. I'm ready to run – I'm
sliding my right foot round towards the front door. But then he
stops, turning towards the cake on the cooling rack.

Mum and I both watch, neither of us daring to breathe – as
he begins to cut the round, golden cake with the knife. What is
he doing? What the heck is he doing?

He cuts right across it – so the cake is in two halves. In an

163

instant he has one half in each hand and – WHAM! I have hot cake pressed against my face, crumbling up my nose, filling my mouth; I can't breathe, I can't see – I'm choking, my face is burning. He keeps pressing until there is no cake, only crumbs, down my neck, and falling from me, covering the floor, and his hand, only his big, hot hand, smothering my face. I stumble backwards, away, coughing, clutching my face, rubbing my eyes. When I can open them, I see Mum has slid down and is sitting on the floor, doing the same.

Why hadn't I run when I had the chance? Why had I stood there like an idiot and watched him cut the cake – let him humiliate us both like this?

I turn and run upstairs. I shut my bedroom door. My music is still on. I shake the crumbs from my clothes. My hands are shaking too – I don't want them to be but they are. I smell of cake. My skin is burning. I want to wash – but that would mean going downstairs to the bathroom.

Maybe I should call the police. But what could I say? Dad attacked me and Mum with a sponge cake. I can hear their fits of laughter now. But it's not funny. It's not funny.

The next day, I go to the street party for the Queen's Silver Jubilee. I don't want to – but Mum makes me go. I walk aimlessly up and down the long tables, piled with food, but I don't eat any cake.

NineTeen

Leah had mixed feelings as the car turned into their street and the house at the end of the terrace came into view. But immediately she saw that there was something different about it.

'The tarpaulin!' she cried. 'It's gone. The wall – Mum! Dad's done it! We've got a wall!'

'Good on him,' Mum said cheerfully. 'He must have been working all hours!'

Dad was clearly happy to see them and proudly showed off his work. With the wall complete, he'd even started fitting out the kitchen with units.

After the initial excitement, Leah found a sense of dread returning as she climbed the stairs. This house was no good. Bad things had happened here. Dad was wasting his time. He could never make it OK.

As she reached her room she almost expected to find it changed, with the bed round the other way as Mark said he'd had it – and with Mark lying on it, having taken over her room in her absence, reclaimed it for himself. But it was untouched – just as she'd left it. There was no sign that Mark had been there while she was gone.

He didn't come that night either. She began to wonder if he would. She thought about the last time, when she had got angry and thrown the Argos catalogue at him. Maybe she'd scared him off. Maybe he'd never come back.

But he had to come. She needed to talk to him. She needed to tell him about his dad and his new family. Even if he didn't want to listen, she had to tell him.

'Where've you been?' Mark said sharply.

It was three nights later – and there he was, standing by her bed, looking cross.

'Away,' said Leah. 'I am allowed to go away, you know.' She sat up and rubbed her eyes. 'Anyway, where've *you* been?'

'Me?' said Mark. 'I got fed up with coming and you not being here so I thought I'd give it a break. It's an effort – getting here, you know. You could have told me you were going away.'

'I didn't know I was going when I last saw you. Anyway – I've been wanting to see you. I've got something to tell you.'

'Me too,' said Mark.

'Really? What?' Leah asked in surprise.

Mark sat down on the bed and looked into her eyes. 'I've found out about Nathan,' he said.

Leah froze. *Nathan.*

She hadn't even known the boy's name until afterwards. Then the name had been everywhere – in the local papers, on everyone's lips. She didn't want to talk about this. She wanted to talk about Chris – about Jade and Megan. Mark couldn't do this – he couldn't. But curiosity got the better of her. How had he found out? What did he know?

'How...?' she began quietly.

'Like you,' Mark said smugly, 'I've been doing my research. If you weren't going to tell me I thought I'd better find out for myself. There was a letter in that drawer with your old address on it.'

'You've been going through my stuff?' Leah protested.

Mark shrugged. 'You've been going through mine – haven't you?'

'But that's different. You're...'

'Dead? Yeah,' said Mark. 'So I can't go round asking people. But you showed me how to use the internet, didn't you? I put your address in Google. Your old road came up – articles from local papers – about Nathan. I know everything about...'

'No!' Leah cried. 'Stop! If you know, then you know. I know too. So there's no need to talk about it, OK? There's no point.'

167

Mark opened his mouth to speak and Leah feared he was going to protest so she jumped in quickly.

'Anyway – don't you want to hear what I found out? It's about your dad.'

Mark's eyes twitched. 'I know about my dad,' he said. 'So if you know about him, we don't need to talk about it, do we?' His voice was sarcastic, mimicking hers. 'There's no point.'

'I don't think you know this,' said Leah. 'It's about his life now.'

'Now?' said Mark. His smug expression dropped and he frowned. 'What about it?'

'I've seen where he's living. I've seen him – your dad.'

'So?'

'He's living with a woman with two children, two girls. They're twelve and six years old.'

'My dad?' said Mark.

'Yes – Chris Hystaff,' said Leah, nodding.

Mark looked as stunned as she had felt moments earlier.

'Why did you have to tell me that?' he said, suddenly angry. 'I don't want to know. I don't want to know!'

'But are they in danger?' Leah asked. 'I'm worried about them. Do you think he'd . . .'

But Mark had gone.

They *were* in danger from Chris. Mark hadn't said it as such – but he hadn't denied it. She had to do something.

But what could she do? She lay in bed, tossing and turning. Sleep was impossible. In the end, she grabbed a notepad and sat in bed, trying to write a letter to Jade.

Dear Jade,

I'm sorry I upset you last week when we'd been getting on so well. I really like you. You were right though; there was another reason why I was interested in your family. It's to do with Chris. I didn't know how to tell you which is why I didn't say anything at the time. It's not easy to even write it as I don't know if you'll believe me – but I wouldn't say it if it wasn't true. Please, please, believe me. You and your mum and Megan are in danger. Chris Hystaff is bad news.

He has been married before like you said, but he had a son, that he hasn't told you about. And get this, right – I know it'll be hard to believe and it'll be a shock – but I know it's true and I'm only telling you because I don't want anything to happen to you. Chris murdered his son and probably his first wife too – and then he covered it up – pretended they'd just moved away.

I don't know if you've seen him being violent – but even it hasn't happened yet, it could happen any time. I can't tell you how I know – but I'm telling you, I swear it's true. Please believe me. I had to warn you.

Make sure you destroy this letter and that Chris

doesn't see it. Call me when you get a chance – away
from the house.

Take care,

Love Leah

Leah read the letter over and over. To send it or not to
send it? she asked herself. What would it achieve except
to make Jade scared – and then Chris might realise she
knew something and force it out of her. Leah could be
putting them in more danger – and that's assuming
Jade believed her. What if she didn't and she showed
the letter to Chris, telling him how crazy her new
would-be friend had turned out to be?

If only there was someone Leah could talk to about
it. She put the letter in the bedside drawer. She'd look
at it again in the morning.

The next day, Leah reread her letter but she still
didn't have the courage to send it. Instead, she put it in
an envelope and tucked it into the side pocket of her
school bag.

Twenty

At school, Nikki was surprisingly friendly, asking her all about her trip.

'Jess was really put out when I told her you'd gone away,' said Nikki, grinning. 'She's missed you – she doesn't stop asking about you. You'll have to come round soon!'

Leah wondered if Nikki had missed her too. She began to chew over the idea of talking to Nikki. She had to talk to someone. Nikki was the only friend she had.

At lunch time, when Nikki came up to her, smiling warmly, Leah decided to take the plunge. 'Can I talk to you about something serious?' she asked.

Nikki looked surprised – but pleased too. 'Yeah – let's go and sit on that bench.'

'What's up?' said Nikki.

'First – will you promise not to tell anyone else?'

'Sure – what is it?'

'It's to do with Mark Hystaff – you're going to think I'm nuts when I tell you.'

'Go on.'

Leah twiddled her hair nervously between her fingers. 'I think he's dead. I think his dad murdered him – and his mum. I don't think they moved away at all.'

Nikki stared at her open-mouthed. 'But Leah...'

'You haven't been able to find him, have you?' said Leah.

'No, but—'

'And no new school in Scotland asked for his records,' Leah butted in. 'Then there are the clothes that my dad found in the loft – Mark's jeans, his shoes and some of his mum's clothes too. And there's the cassette. And your dad said they were trying to leave secretly. There's nothing to prove that they ever got away.'

'But murder!' said Nikki. 'I mean – all that's a long way from proving they were murdered, isn't it?'

'The thing is,' said Leah. 'While I was away, I found Mark's dad.'

'You what?'

Leah told Nikki all about Jade and Megan and their mum.

'So there was no sign that anything was wrong – that he was beating them up or anything?' Nikki asked, when she'd finished.

'No. Megan had bruises but I think they were from ice-skating. I saw her fall on the ice. But what if something happens to them? What if they get hurt? I feel like I've got to do something. I've written this letter to Jade.'

'You can't send this,' Nikki told Leah firmly when she'd finished reading. 'You'll terrify her – and what if you're wrong?'

'But I've got to do something,' Leah protested. 'What else can I do?'

'I know you believe what you're telling me is what happened,' Nikki said gently. 'But don't you think . . . maybe your imagination might be getting carried away? I mean, once you got the idea in your head – it's kept going round and round and it feels real but actually it's not at all.'

'It's true, I know it's true,' said Leah. 'I can't stop thinking about it. I couldn't concentrate at all this morning.'

She felt tears well up unexpectedly and they began to slide down her cheeks before she could stop them.

'You're in a right state, aren't you? Maybe you should see the counsellor,' said Nikki.

'That's what Mum's friend, Kate, said,' Leah sniffed.

'You told her all this?'

'No – no. She could see the state I was in, that's all.'

'Well, I think she had the right idea,' said Nikki. 'Come on, I'll come with you to the office and make an appointment.'

Leah found herself following Nikki inside and along the corridor.

'But what about Jade and Megan?' Leah said. 'I've got to warn them somehow, haven't I?'

'No, you don't,' said Nikki. 'If you're really that worried, you can go to the police. Let them look into it properly. Hey, maybe they'll even find Mark! That'd put your mind at rest and there'd be a double bonus 'cause he could come to Dad's reunion!'

'The police?' said Leah. 'You're right, that's what I should do. It's obvious, now you said it. I'll go after school. Nikki – will you... will you come with me?'

'I don't know...' Nikki fidgeted and frowned, then met Leah's eyes. 'Yeah, I guess so, if you want me to...'

'Thanks, Nikki. I feel much better now. I don't think I need to see the counsellor at all. You've helped me. I'm fine now.'

Nikki shook her head. 'I still think you should see her.'

'I'll see how I feel tomorrow,' said Leah. 'I can make an appointment then if I need it.'

'All right.'

'Thanks,' said Leah.

'Ah – girls! Just the two I was looking for!' Mrs Keeble came hurrying up to them. 'I'm hoping you will give me a hand down in the archives,' she said.

Leah saw Nikki's shoulders droop. How could they get out of this?

'I found something I think might interest you,' Mrs Keeble added.

This was enough to get Leah immediately to her feet. 'Coming, Miss,' she said.

She looked round. Nikki was following.

'It's the punishment book from 1978,' said Mrs Keeble, as they reached the bottom of the stairs.

'Punishment book?' said Leah.

'Yes – that boy, Mark Hystaff, that you were interested in, he was one of the last pupils at this school to be caned before the cane was banned.'

'Caned!' Leah exclaimed. 'But that's inhumane! It sounds like something from the 1800s, not the 1970s. What had he done?'

Mrs Keeble picked up an old book with a dusty blue cover and turned the pages. 'Here – see?'

Leah scanned the page. There were lists of names, and columns with the crime and the punishment. The crimes included rudeness, talking in class, disobedience, late homework, throwing a chair. The punishment column was mainly detentions but one boy had been suspended for one week. One girl had had a hundred lines and one boy the cane.

That was Mark's entry.

'Fighting?' said Leah, reading it. 'He was caned for fighting. That doesn't sound like Mark.'

She turned to Nikki, who shrugged in agreement.

'It looks like it was the only time,' said Mrs Keeble, flicking through the earlier pages.

'I'll ask my dad about it,' said Nikki. 'He never

175

mentioned anything like that.'

'Now,' said Mrs Keeble, smiling, 'if you'd like to sort through these for me from the 1980s, that would be very handy.' She was pointing to two very full boxes of papers.

Leah glanced at Nikki who raised her eyebrows as if this was the last thing she wanted to do. But they both crouched down and began to lift the papers from the boxes.

Twenty-one

Outside the police station, Leah hesitated.

'Go on – in you go,' said Nikki. She pushed the door for Leah, but clearly didn't want to go in first.

Leah took a deep breath and went through the door. She glanced round at the three chairs against the side wall. Two were empty, one occupied by a shabbily dressed man with his legs outstretched and a fixed scowl on his face.

Nikki gave her a gentle push towards the counter, where no one was visible. Leah wasn't sure. Was this man first? He looked like he might get angry if she jumped the queue.

At that moment a policewoman appeared behind the counter. She gave Leah and Nikki a patronising smile but seemed to be ignoring the man and expecting Leah to come forward. Leah approached the desk, her fingers tingling with nerves. She wished the man wasn't there. He was making her uncomfortable.

'Yes?' said the policewoman.

Leah leaned forward, speaking quietly. 'It's ... it's about a murder – one that happened a long time ago.' She felt an anxious flutter in her stomach as she spoke.

The policewoman leaned back, looking her up and down as if unsure whether to take her seriously. She had probably been expecting Leah to report a stolen mobile phone or something like that.

'It might not be a murder,' Nikki chipped in. 'She doesn't know for sure – it might be more of a missing person kind of thing.'

Leah felt cross – almost wishing Nikki hadn't come. It would be hard enough to convince the police to take her seriously, without Nikki adding to their doubts.

'I'll need to take a few details then,' said the police-woman. She picked up a pen and pulled a large notepad across. 'Tell me what you know.'

Leah shuffled awkwardly, looking round at the man who was still sitting behind them.

'Can't we – talk somewhere more private?' Leah asked quietly.

'You'll have to have a parent present if we are going to interview you properly,' said the policewoman. 'Just give me a few details and I'll pass them on to CID. They'll decide if the matter needs investigating and arrange for you to come in with a parent if necessary.'

Leah gulped. She could imagine Mum or Dad's reaction. She wanted to turn round and leave now – but the policewoman was twiddling her pen expectantly.

Leah looked at Nikki, who gave her a reassuring smile.

'It happened in my house – the house where I'm living now,' Leah began – but as she spoke she was startled by the sound of a swinging door. She turned to see a woman coming out of a room into the foyer area. The man who'd been sitting stood up and greeted her – and they both left quickly. Leah was relieved. At least he wouldn't be listening in.

'Carry on,' said the policewoman impatiently.

'Yes,' said Leah. 'This man – he lived in the house – years ago – and he murdered his son and his wife – only no one knows. The thing is, I know who he is and where he's living now – and he's got a new partner and she's got children. That's why I'm telling you – I'm scared he might do something to them too.'

'Perhaps you can tell me the names of the people involved and exactly when this happened,' said the policewoman. 'Then CID can check the files.'

Leah told her the names and that the year was 1979. 'But I don't know if there'll be anything in your files,' Leah added. 'Mark's dad, Chris Hystaff – he told everyone his wife had left him and taken Mark with her. No one knew he'd actually killed them.'

'And what makes you think that he *did* kill them?' the policewoman asked.

Leah told her about the *Top of the Pops* cassette; about the school records not being requested; about Mark's friend Simon not having heard from him again and not being able to track him down now for the reunion. Then she told her about the clothes in the loft.

'That's quite a list,' said the policewoman, 'but in my mind, there's nothing in all that to suggest that they were actually murdered. You could bring the clothes in and we'll take a look if you like.'

Leah's heart sank. 'But I don't have them any more. They stank. My dad chucked them out.'

'Well, in that case,' said the policewoman, shaking her head, 'I don't think there's much to go on.'

'Is there a way you can find out?' Nikki interjected. 'I mean, if Mark and his mum did move away like his dad said, then is there a way you can track down where they went – or where they are now?'

'If we had a reason to find them, then there might be,' said the policewoman, 'but the police don't really have time to go round looking for people whom no one has reported missing to make sure that no one murdered them thirty years ago.'

Leah could see the woman was losing interest.

'Maybe they *were* reported missing,' said Leah. 'If they were going to stay with someone – a relative in Scotland, that person might have reported them missing when they didn't arrive. Could you at least check that?'

'Yes – of course – I will pass the details on to DC Wallace in CID. She'll check missing persons and see if we have anything else on file. That's all I can do at the moment. All right? DC Wallace will be in touch if she wants to talk to you further. And if you have any more substantial information, you can contact her directly – this is her number.' She scribbled something on a small card and held it out. Then she turned away.

That was it then.

'Maybe they will have something on file,' said Nikki, as they walked down the road. 'You never know.'

But Leah knew Nikki didn't really believe it. At least if the police found nothing, then Mum or Dad wouldn't have to get involved. Leah would have to find out more herself – something that would be proof – so that the police and Mum and Dad would have to take her seriously.

'Will you go and see the counsellor?' Nikki asked. 'I still think it would be a good idea.'

'I might. I'll see how I feel tomorrow,' said Leah.

'Do you want to come back to mine?' Nikki asked.

Leah shook her head. 'I think I'll go home if you don't mind.'

'No worries. Why don't you come round tomorrow after school? We can work on that history and I know Jess is dying to see you.'

'OK. Thanks for coming with me,' said Leah.

As they parted and Leah walked towards her house, she felt numb. How could she get the proof about Mark? How could she make anyone believe her when the best evidence she had was a ghost in her bedroom? What if something happened to Jade and Megan?

Back at home, her dad met her in the hallway.

'Leah – I don't understand how you can go out and leave your music on full pelt upstairs!' he said crossly. 'And it's a right mess up there.'

'It wasn't me,' Leah protested.

'What do you mean, *it wasn't you?* Don't be so ridiculous! Who else do you think has been up there?'

'Dad . . .'

'Tttt.' Dad turned and walked away before Leah could say anything. Not that she knew what she was going to say.

As she tidied her room she spoke aloud to Mark. She had no idea if he could hear her.

'You can't keep doing this,' she told him. 'It's not fair. You're getting me in trouble. Are you there? Can you hear me? You've got to stop this!'

'Leah?'

She looked up. Mum was in the doorway.

'Mum – you're early!'

'My meeting finished early,' said Mum. She looked hard at Leah. 'Leah – who were you talking to just now?'

'Just to myself,' Leah said, shrugging.

'I am getting seriously worried about you,' said Mum. 'Kate was concerned but I kept telling her you were

OK. Now I'm not so sure. Is there anything you want to talk about?'

The way Mum said it, Leah sensed she was scared of what Leah might say. She knew she couldn't talk to Mum – ever.

'I'm going to see the school counsellor,' she told her.

Mum's shoulders sank in relief. 'Really?'

Leah nodded. 'Yes, tomorrow. So you don't need to worry.'

'Good – I think that's a good idea. Let me know how it goes.'

'I will.'

The next day, Leah sat in the counsellor's room, her arms folded tight, eyes on the floor.

The counsellor sat opposite, her legs crossed, waiting. 'This time is yours; you can talk to me about anything that's on your mind.'

Leah glanced up briefly. The counsellor, Marion, was a small woman with large dangling earrings. She had a warm smile and kind eyes.

'I don't know where to start,' Leah said quietly.

'Say the first thing that comes into your head,' Marion suggested.

'I saw them bring Nathan out,' Leah found herself saying. She didn't know why she said it – she hadn't expected to. That wasn't why she'd come at all – but now she'd started she couldn't stop. 'I saw. No one knows that. They think I stayed in the house, like they told me – but I came out. I saw...'

Leah let out a big gulping sob. What was going on? Why had she started about Nathan?

'Nathan?' said Marion.

'He was the boy in the fire,' said Leah. 'It was next door... the house next door to our old house. It was six months ago.'

'Do you want to tell me what happened – what you saw?'

Leah wanted to say 'no' – that she didn't want to talk about it – but suddenly she found she was talking.

'It was awful – Dad woke in the night and smelled the smoke. He went out the front and saw the smoke and the flames next door. He called 999. The woman got out – Nathan's mum – and she was screaming that her son was in there.

'I came out to see what was going on – even though Mum and Dad told me to stay inside. I saw Dad go in – I thought he was going to die. He didn't think about it – he just went straight in. It seemed like ages – then he was carrying him out, Nathan – they were both black with smoke – and he laid him down on the ground. I thought it was his clothes hanging off him – Nathan – but then I realised it was his skin.'

'His skin?'

'On his legs – just hanging off like it was a bit of

material. You could see his bone – I think. I think I saw his bone.'

'That must have been horrific,' said Marion.

Leah gulped another sob. 'I thought he was dead – so did his mum. She was crying and screaming. But the fire brigade came then and the ambulance. They said he wasn't dead. He was alive. They took him to hospital. At the hospital they said he should be OK. He'd have to have skin grafts and operations but he would be OK. Everyone said Dad was a hero – that he'd saved the boy's life.'

'It sounds like your dad was very brave,' said Marion.

'He was,' said Leah, 'but he could have been killed. The firefighters said he was very lucky to get away with minor burns on his hands and a sore throat from the smoke. They say people should wait for them to arrive and not go into burning buildings because it's too dangerous. They have the proper equipment and everything. But Dad didn't know that. He was brave to go in there like he did.'

'So what happened next?' asked Marion.

'Nathan's mum came round to our place a few days later and she was hugging Dad and crying. She was so grateful to him. She said they didn't have a smoke alarm so they didn't know about the fire until it was too late.

'She told us Nathan was in a lot of pain – but that he was alive and he would be OK. But he wasn't. He had lung damage from the smoke – much worse than they thought – and his lungs started to pack in. Gradually he got worse and worse. It took him three weeks to die.'

'It must have been very upsetting for you. Did you know Nathan well before all this?'

'No – they'd only just moved in. I didn't even know his name. I'd seen him in the street, that's all. He was the same age as me – he was going to start at this school. I didn't know him at all – but I kind of…I kind of liked the look of him, if you know what I mean. I thought we were going to get on. The day before it happened, he'd waved at me when he was getting into his mum's car. The way he'd looked at me – I thought, he likes me too. I couldn't wait to meet him properly, to talk to him.'

Leah paused.

'But you never had the chance?' said Marion.

Leah shook her head. 'And it would have been better for Nathan if Dad hadn't gone in – if he'd died quickly in the fire. That's what cut Dad up. He couldn't handle it – it wasn't how it was supposed to be. Dad got himself in a state after Nathan died and then he had a breakdown.'

'That can't seem very fair,' said Marion.

'No – it wasn't fair. It wasn't fair at all. One brave act from Dad and it's ended up messing up our whole lives.'

'And how's your dad now?'

'He's getting better. He's much better.'

'And you've never talked to him about any of this – how it has affected you?'

186

'No – I couldn't. I used to be really close to him – I used to tell him everything.'

'He doesn't even know you saw him bring Nathan out?'

'No.'

'Maybe it's time you did talk to him.'

Leah shook her head. 'I don't want to set him back.'

'It's up to you of course – but maybe it would help you both.'

'I'll think about it,' said Leah.

Mark
December 1978
The Winter of Discontent

I pick up the phone. My hand is shaking as I dial 9 . . . 9 . . . 9. He's killing her. I'm sure he's killing her. She's screaming from the front room, begging him to stop. She sounds like a little kid, a helpless little kid.

I tried begging him, too – 'Stop! Please stop!'

She was shaking her head – motioning at me to go. I don't know if she meant me to call the police – but when HE gave me that snide look, eyes shining with power, and said, 'Stop? You mean, stop THIS?' and punched her hard in the stomach so she keeled over, I walked out, came to the phone in the hall.

Why is no one answering? Is it because of the strikes? I don't know why but there's loads of strikes going on. They're calling it the winter of discontent. The dustmen haven't been and there's rubbish piled up in the street. It stinks. Life stinks. The country is falling apart.

The police can't be on strike, can they? I panic – but at last I'm through. I ask for police. A woman questions me. I stutter as I try to speak. I tell her. She asks me the address. She says

188

the police will come. She tells me to keep out of the room where HE is. She doesn't need to tell me that.

I don't want to put the phone down. She has a nice, kind voice. I want her to stay on the line. But she's gone. I wait. I listen for the siren. Will there be a siren? It feels like an age. They haven't come. Where are they? I look at my watch. Only two minutes have passed. Is that all? But then it's five minutes, ten minutes…

I'm sitting on the stairs. It's gone quiet in the front room. He's stopped. I see Mum go past, head bowed, crying, into the bathroom. I want to follow her but I'm scared to move. HE's still in the front room and I'd have to go past. It's another ten minutes before the police knock at the door. I stay where I am on the stairs, my heart beating like a bass drum.

HE answers it. I hear the surprise in his voice, the slight edge but it's so slight it's gone by the time he's said, 'Can I help you, Officer?'

'We had a report of an incident,' the policeman says.

'I'm afraid you must have got the wrong address,' HE says, so pleasantly, so calmly. 'There's been no incident here.'

'You have a wife and child?' the police officer persists.

'Yes, they're fine,' HE replies. He pauses, then adds, 'You can see for yourself if you like.'

HE's hoping the policeman will go, but the policeman must have nodded because HE calls me, with the same pleasant tone. 'Mark! Come here a minute, will you?'

I come down slowly. HE must know it was me called the police. If they don't take him away, then I'm for it.

I have to be brave. 'It was me called you,' I tell the police-man. 'He was hitting my mum.'

'Nothing of the sort,' HE says. He gives a slight laugh, as if I've said something ridiculous. 'Maggie!'

Mum comes out of the bathroom. Her face looks puffy to me but there's no other immediate sign, nothing obvious. She must be black and blue under those clothes, she must be.

'You all right, love?' the policeman asks. 'Your son here called us, said your husband was being violent.'

Mum says nothing. I silently will her to speak. 'Say some-thing, Mum. Say something and they'll take him away.'

But it's HIM who speaks. 'Just a bit of a row, that's all, Officer,' HE says. 'I do tend to raise my voice a bit when I've got cause. Must've worried the boy. I'm so sorry to have troubled you. Everything's fine now.'

HE sounds so reasonable; he even puts his arm gently round Mum. Doesn't the policeman see her cringe?

'Well, love?' The policeman looks at Mum.

'I'm fine,' Mum says. HIS arm is still round her. 'Nothing to worry about,' she adds.

I am seething. I can't believe it. I can't believe she said that. My heart sinks into my slippers as the door closes behind the policeman. I turn and run up the stairs. I think he'll come after me, knock the living daylights out of me. He doesn't come straight away. I wait – I wait. I know he'll come. He comes.

The next morning, I'm aching like my bones are crushed – and I'm still seething – seething with Mum. When he's left for work, I lay into her.

190

'Why didn't you tell the police? They would have arrested him, put him away for it if they knew. You let him off. You let him do this to me!'

I pull up my top, turn round, show her my back.

She sighs. I turn round and meet her sad, defeated eyes.

'They'd never have charged him,' she says. 'It's only a domestic as far as they're concerned. They might have taken him, questioned him, but he'd have been back, and worse than ever. Don't you see? I don't want to make things any worse.'

I hate her. How can things be any worse? I hate her as much as I hate him. Why does she have to be so weak, so pathetic?

I go to school. Mr Phelps asks me a question in maths. I'm not listening – I guess the answer, say something – but I know instantly it's wrong because everyone's laughing. At break Ricky Wood calls me a moron. The furnace inside me ignites. I explode. Before I know what's happened blood is spurting out of Ricky Wood's mouth and he's lost two front teeth. I'm in big trouble.

I find myself standing in the Head Teacher's office. I'm stubbornly silent. I refuse to try to explain. What can I say? The head, Mr Richards, picks up the cane. He's not going to use it. He just enjoys threatening kids with it. He's hardly ever used it since I've been at the school. They're talking about banning it – it's been on the news. But he's pointing to a chair, telling me to bend over. I look at him, thinking he can't be serious. But he is. He must be having a bad day. He says it again.

'We will not tolerate violence at this school!' he booms.

He doesn't even see the irony in his words. I bend over the

191

chair. It can't hurt me, I tell myself. Nothing can hurt me. I'm hurting too much for any more pain to make any difference.

Twenty-Two

'How did it go?' Nikki asked, as they walked back to Nikki's after school.

'She said I should talk to Dad about the fire; about Nathan,' said Leah.

'You talked to her about all that?' Nikki asked.

Leah nodded.

'Do you know,' said Nikki, 'I've never heard you say those words before – "fire" or his name, "Nathan".'

'I couldn't.'

'Well, that's progress, then, isn't it? She must be doing you some good. What about Mark Hystaff and all this murder stuff? Did you talk about that?'

'I was going to – that's why I went. But somehow the stuff about Nathan and the fire came out first. I don't know why. Then I ran out of time.'

'Leah!'

Jess came running out of the house and flung her arms round Leah, who hugged her back.

'Hi, Jess. I've missed you.'

Jess hugged tighter and Leah lifted her off the ground.

'Have I grown since you came?' Jess demanded.

'It's not that long – only a couple of weeks!' said Leah, putting her down and standing back.

'But Mum says my trousers are too short and that I'm growing every day!' said Jess.

'I'm sure you are,' said Leah, laughing.

'Will you play with me?' Jess begged, pulling Leah into the house. 'Mum! Leah's here!'

'She's a whirlwind, isn't she?' said Nikki, shaking her head. 'Are you sure you can cope with her? If you don't feel like it, don't worry.'

'We'll have a few games and then see if we can escape and get that history done,' said Leah.

'Hi, Leah!' said Nikki's mum. She was holding Ben who gave Leah a lovely smile.

'Ben likes you too, Leah,' said Nikki, laughing. 'What is it with you?'

'Must dash,' said Nikki's mum. 'The pong from this fellow tells me he's in need of a change.'

'Poooh!' cried Jess, clutching her nose. 'Take him away, Mum, quick!'

After a few games with Jess, Nikki was insistent that she and Leah needed to do their homework. At first Jess said she'd help but she soon got bored as they began to discuss the history and she left them in peace.

'I'm glad I've got you for a friend,' Leah told Nikki, when they had finished.

Nikki smiled. 'That's only because I'm a historian extraordinaire and you're going to get A++!' she teased.

'No – really,' said Leah. 'Thanks for listening to me before – and for suggesting about the police and the counsellor.'

'That was nothing,' said Nikki.

As she walked home later, Leah's mobile beeped. It was a message – from Jade! This was a surprise. Leah read it eagerly.

'U got it all wrong about Chris. He's not who U think he is.'

What? What did Jade mean? What did she know? And how? Leah had never sent her letter. If Jade had somehow found out why Leah had been so interested in them, then how did Jade know that Leah was wrong? Maybe the police had been round and questioned Chris and that was how Jade knew. Chris could have somehow convinced them all that it was nothing to do with him.

Leah had a moment's doubt. Had she got it all wrong? Could Chris be innocent? No – she was sure, so sure.

She sent a quick text back. 'What U mean?'

As she reached the house, her phone beeped again. Jade had replied, 'Stay away & leave us alone.'

She put her phone away as she reached the house.

Once outside, Dad told her Mum was going to be late.

Leah pushed Jade out of her mind. There was something else she had to do and now seemed like the perfect opportunity.

'Dad, can we have a talk?' she asked.

They sat on the sofa bed.

Leah was quiet. Was this really such a good idea?

'Spit it out then,' said Dad.

'I saw the counsellor at school today,' said Leah. 'I don't want to upset you, but she says I should talk to you about – talk about what happened with – with Nathan. I know you're much better now – but is it OK to talk about it? I won't if it will still upset you . . . '

Leah felt herself mumbling.

Dad moved closer and squeezed her hand. 'We've never talked about it, have we, not properly? You say whatever you need to say.'

'I saw more than you think,' said Leah.

Dad frowned. 'What do you mean?'

'When it happened – the smell of burning and we came outside and saw the fire,' said Leah, 'you and Mum told me to go back in the house. I went – but I came out again. In all the chaos, Mum didn't see me. But I saw you go in, Dad. I saw you go into that burning house. I thought you were going to die. It seemed like forever that you were in there. And then I saw you bring Nathan out.'

'You saw all that?' Dad sounded flabbergasted. 'But you never said.'

'I couldn't talk about it,' said Leah, 'and then, after he died, you…'

'I cracked up,' filled in Dad.

'Yes – and it was even harder,' said Leah.

Dad pulled her close. She rested her head on his warm, broad chest.

'Oh, Leah. No wonder you're in a state. Once I went to pieces, all the focus was on me. I was terrified in there. I tell you, Leah – I thought I was going to die too. But I'd seen that boy's mother's face. I was determined to get him out. And when they said he was alive – I thought I'd done it. It was so hard when he died. I couldn't take it.'

'You tried though,' said Leah. 'You tried to save him – that's what counts.'

'That's what everyone kept saying – but I just couldn't see it myself – not then. I'd failed – he was dead. If I'd been quicker – if I'd done something differently…'

'It wouldn't have changed anything,' said Leah.

'That's probably true – but you – you've been bottling it all up. I'm so sorry, Leah – I'm sure you must be angry with me.'

'Angry?'

'I should have been stronger,' said Dad. 'I shouldn't have fallen apart over it. I was hell to live with, I know. And we had to move – I couldn't stay there, next to that burnt out house. It messed up your life, I know it did.'

'It wasn't your fault,' said Leah. 'I'm proud that you went in there – you were so brave. You didn't deserve what happened after – what do they call it?'

'Post Traumatic Stress Disorder,' said Dad.

'Yes – that. It wasn't fair.'

Dad squeezed her hand. 'The house is coming on, isn't it? I'll have it finished soon. We'll build ourselves up again.'

'Dad . . .'

'Yes – go on.'

'Do you believe in ghosts?'

Dad's eyebrows shot up. 'Where's that come from all of a sudden?'

'Seriously, Dad, just answer the question,' said Leah.

'Actually – when I was a child, after my grandma died, I remember waking up in the night and seeing her – right there, sitting on my bed. And when she turned to go, I saw that she had wings. I'm sure it was a dream – but you never know! You're not going to start telling me this house is haunted, are you?' He chuckled.

Leah met his eyes. His smile dropped.

'There is a ghost here,' she said quietly.

'Who? Nathan?' said Dad.

'No – it's not Nathan – it's—'

The phone began to ring and Dad jumped up to answer it. 'That'll be your mum, saying she's going to be even later,' said Dad, sighing.

But it wasn't Mum. It was Nikki. Dad handed the phone to Leah.

'Guess what?' said Nikki. She sounded excited.

'What?' said Leah.

'Dad's found Mark!' said Nikki.

'What?' Leah said again.

'Dad's found Mark,' Nikki repeated, 'alive and well in London!'

'But it's not possible . . .' said Leah. 'How?'

'It wouldn't be possible if your mad theory was right and he was dead, would it? But he's not dead – he's alive. Dad's been asking the old school mates he's found on *Friends Reunited* if they know what happened to Mark – and someone called Terry said yes! He'd kept in touch and seen him now and then. He last saw him about a month ago. He's asked him if he'll come to the reunion and he said he will!'

'Leah?'

'Leah – are you still there?'

Twenty-Three

Leah lay restlessly awake all night. Jade said she was wrong. Nikki said she was wrong. But the ghost of Mark meant something else. If he was a ghost, then he couldn't be alive, could he? Nothing made sense any more – nothing at all.

'Can I see this email – the one your dad got from Terry about Mark?' Leah asked Nikki, at school the next day.

'If you want,' said Nikki, shrugging. 'I thought you'd be pleased, Leah. You thought he was dead and he's not. I don't know why you're so upset.'

'I just want to be completely sure that it's him,' said Leah.

'Fine – come back to mine after school and I'll show you.'

Back at Nikki's, Leah waited while Nikki brought the email up on the screen.

'Look – here,' she told Leah, pointing.

Leah read it. *'You asked if I remember Mark. I do. We've kept in touch. We see each other now and then. He's living in London – works for an IT company – ZoneFuture, I think it's called. I saw him last month as a matter of fact. He's divorced – got three kids that he sees at weekends. I'll let him know about the reunion – I'm sure he'll want to come. Anyone else you want me to contact?'*

'There you go,' said Nikki. 'Do you believe it now?'

Leah nodded half-heartedly. It couldn't be him, could it? She knew that. 'Did he change his name or is it still Hystaff?' she asked.

Nikki shrugged. 'I don't know – but Terry called him and said Mark's definitely coming to the reunion.'

Back at home Leah looked up 'ZoneFuture' on the internet. It was there but no individual names were listed. Leah wrote down the phone number.

After school the next day, she phoned it.

'Hello. Can I speak to Mark Hystaff?' she asked, nervously.

'Mark who?' said a woman's voice.

'Mark – he works there. I think his name's Hystaff but I may have got that wrong. You do have a Mark working there, don't you?'

'Hold on.'

Leah waited. She didn't know how big the company was. Maybe there'd be three or four Marks there and she wouldn't know which one.

'Putting you through,' said the woman.

'Hello, Mark Peters here. Can I help you?'

Leah felt a flutter of panic. What was she going to say?

'Hello. Who am I speaking to?' asked Mark Peters.

'Hi. My name's Leah,' said Leah. 'I'm helping Simon Taylor to organise the reunion for Fairmead School. I just wanted to check something with you.'

'The reunion – yes, Terry told me about that. I've already said I'll come.'

'Yes – I know. I just wanted to ask you – was your last name always Peters or did it used to be Hystaff?'

'Hystaff? No, that's not me. You must be confusing me with someone – ahh – hang on, come to think of it, there was another Mark in our year at school for a while. He left – long before O levels. Maybe that's the Hystaff one. He was friendly with Simon, I seem to remember. Did Simon think I was him?'

'I think he might have done,' said Leah.

'That makes sense,' said Mark. 'I did wonder when Terry said Simon was so keen to find me. It seemed odd as I never knew Simon well at all.'

'You didn't keep in touch with him – this other Mark, did you?' asked Leah.

'No – he wasn't a mate of mine either. I wouldn't have remembered he existed if you hadn't said the name Hystaff.'

'Thank you – that's very helpful,' said Leah.

Leah went round to Nikki's. Upstairs in Nikki's room, she told her what she'd found out.

'You phoned up ZoneFuture and spoke to him?' Nikki said in surprise.

'I was sure he couldn't be Mark Hystaff,' said Leah, nodding, 'so I had to sort it out.'

'Dad will be so disappointed,' said Nikki. 'It would have been dead embarrassing if they hadn't realised until the reunion! But I can't understand why you were so sure it wasn't him. I know you think Mark is dead – but there's no absolute proof, is there?'

She looked Leah hard in the face so that Leah had to turn her eyes away. 'Is there?' she repeated. 'Leah – you know something, don't you? There's something you're not telling me.'

Leah shrugged. 'There is something – but I can't tell you what it is. I do know he's dead – that's all I can say.'

'You've got to tell me,' said Nikki. 'What is it? How do you know? You can't expect me to just accept that without explaining.'

Leah bit her lip nervously.

'Come on, Leah. Spit it out!' Nikki urged.

'Do you believe in ghosts?' Leah asked.

'*Ghosts!*' Nikki's face contorted in surprise. She tried to conceal a snort. 'You're not trying to say...?'

'Yes,' Leah snapped. 'I know Mark's dead because

I've seen his ghost – I've talked to him too. You don't have to believe me but it's true. OK?'

'Leah – you're even more messed up than I thought,' said Nikki, shaking her head. 'When are you seeing that counsellor again?'

'I'm not seeing her again,' said Leah. 'There's no point, is there? I'm certainly not telling her about this – she won't believe me any more than you or anyone else. She'll send me off to a psychiatrist and they'll say I'm having hallucinations or something and dose me up with drugs.'

'Didn't your dad see a psychiatrist?' asked Nikki. 'I mean, they helped him, didn't they?'

'That was different – he was ill, he was traumatised. I'm not. There's nothing wrong with me. I've just seen a ghost – a real ghost, that's all. I know Mark is dead. You wanted to know how I knew and I've told you. I'm going now.'

As Leah headed for the stairs, she heard the doorbell ring.

'That's my grandparents,' said Nikki, following. 'They've had Jess for the afternoon.'

Leah ignored her and started down the stairs.

'Leah – wait,' said Nikki.

Nikki's mum was opening the door. Jess burst in and seeing Leah her face lit up and she was up the stairs and wrapping herself round Leah before Leah had a chance to move or speak.

Leah hugged Jess back stiffly.

'Why didn't you tell me you were coming?' Jess demanded.

'I didn't know in advance,' said Leah. 'It's nice to see you, Jess, but actually, I'm going now.'

Jess looked up at her in astonishment. 'You can't go now. That's not fair! Anyway – Nana and Grandpa want to meet you! It'll be rude if you go, won't it, Mum?'

'You're welcome to stay, Leah,' said Nikki's mum, smiling. 'At least come and have a cup of tea with us – unless you need to rush off for something, of course?'

Jess clung to her tight.

'Sorry, I do have to go, actually,' said Leah, unravelling herself from Jess's arms.

'No, Leah, stay!' Jess squealed.

'I've got to go,' said Leah. 'I'll see you another time.'

She said a quick uncomfortable goodbye to Nikki and left.

It was starting to get dark as she reached her street. In the distance, she thought she saw a man standing outside her house, looking up at it – but as she got nearer the person had vanished. Did they have a visitor?

As she came into the house, the lights were on but there was an eerie silence.

'Dad?' she called.

He didn't answer, but she was shocked to find him sitting on the new kitchen floor, his back against the wall at the end of the row of new cabinet frames. His legs were stretched out and his head was in his hands.

'Dad! What's happened? Was it someone at the door just now? What did they want?'

'At the door?' he muttered, slowly moving his hands. 'There was no one at the door.'

'I thought I saw someone outside,' said Leah. 'What's happened? What's the matter?'

'It's too much, all this,' said Dad. 'I wish I'd never started.'

Leah wished it too. She wished it more than anything. But her own feelings, the turmoil in her head didn't matter right now. She couldn't bear to see Dad like this.

'But you're getting on really well,' said Leah. She crouched on the floor beside him. 'Come on, get up and I'll make us a drink.'

'The units aren't the right size,' said Dad, his eyes glazed over. 'I've fitted all that lot and now I've got to take them all out, take out the sink and start over again.'

'I'm not surprised you're fed up,' said Leah. 'But it's not the end of the world. It'll get done.'

'Yes – but it's muggins here who's got to do it, isn't it? Andy and Dave can't spare me any more time right now.'

'Why?'

'They've got another job to go on to – one that pays more. This has taken far longer than we thought. I'm sorry, love. I shouldn't be bothering you with all this.'

Leah reached out her hand. 'Come on – get up. We can't have Mum coming home finding you like this.'

'She should leave,' said Dad. 'Both of you – you and your mum – you should just go. You'll be better off without me.'

'Stop talking rubbish!' Leah cried angrily. 'If Mum was going to leave she'd have done it by now. She loves you – so do I. We'll stick by you, Dad.'

Dad squeezed Leah's hand and eased himself up.

'This isn't because of me,' said Leah, 'talking about Nathan and...'

'No – no. It's not that at all. You were right to talk to me. I'm glad you did. No – it's the kitchen that's getting me down. But you're right. It's not the end of the world.'

'I'll help you if you like,' said Leah.

'Thanks, Leah. You're a good kid. I'm lucky to have you.'

Mark
Leaving

I'm twelve years old and I'm lying on my bed with my music on loud – too loud. Mum's in the doorway, pointing at the stereo and making faces at me to turn it down. I don't want to. The music is the only way I survive. It blocks out everything else – and HE's at work – so what does it matter? But Mum's getting impatient. She's over by the stereo, fiddling with the dials before I can stop her.

'Leave it. I'll do it! I'll do it!' I yell. But the music's gone. Dead.

'It's all right. It's done,' says Mum.

That's when I think, this is weird. There's something different about her. She doesn't usually mess with my stereo. She's been looking so small lately – like she's shrinking. I don't know if it's because I'm getting taller or because of HIM. I'm not that tall. I think it's since the hospital – she's been kind of bent over. It was her ribs. He didn't want to take her to hospital – couldn't risk it after the last time when they started asking questions. Mum was begging. I was begging too. She was in agony. In the end he took her to a different hospital, in a *different town.*

Anyway, I think it got Mum scared. She knows the next time he might not take her at all. Then what will she do? I wish I could do something to stop him. I'm thinking about doing weight training and boxing on the sly. Then one day I'll surprise him.

'Come on, we're leaving,' says Mum.

I frown at her. She's got this wild look in her eyes. She's standing straight, not bent over.

'What?'

'We're going. We're getting out of here, you and me – for good. Come on, before your dad gets home.'

'But where?' I feel a pounding in my stomach.

'Never mind where. Come on.'

She pulls my sports bag out of the wardrobe. I see her flinch with pain and clutch her ribs. 'Pack a few things in there – the bare essentials, mind.'

I look around my room, panicking. 'But what about my stereo, my records?'

'We can't carry everything, can we? Hurry up.'

'But when did you decide? Why didn't you give me some warning? We can't just leave...'

'For God's sake, Mark!' Mum's voice is so fierce, so unlike her, I shut up. I've been wanting this so long – wanting to get out of here – wanting her to have the guts to leave HIM – and now, now it's real, I feel paralysed. I can't move.

Mum is at my chest of drawers, opening my underwear drawer, thrusting pants into the sports bag. I stand up giddily *and grab my favourite jumper from the back of the chair.*

'Are we really never coming back?' I whisper.

'Never.'

'But I need to tell Simon. What will he think if I've just gone?'

'Mark – if we're going to do this, we've just got to do it, OK? I've had enough. I can't take any more. That man has worn us both into the ground. He's destroying us. I don't care about me. But he's destroying you – and I'm not going to let that happen.'

'But Mum...'

'Enough!' Her voice is firm. 'You've got all you need? Let's go.'

That's when the phone rings. Mum looks at me. The phone hardly ever rings in our house – unless it's him, checking up on us.

'Come on. I'm not going to answer it,' says Mum.

The ringing stops.

I feel a sudden urgent need to pee. 'I've got to go to the loo,' I say. 'I won't be a sec.'

Mum looks impatient. I run down the stairs to the bathroom. I can't believe this is happening. I can't believe we're actually going.

As I reach up to pull the chain, I hear the phone ring again. I come out. I can hear Mum talking. She's answered it. My heart sinks. She said she wouldn't and she has. I'm about to wrench the phone out of her hand. But Mum's talking in a formal voice – so it's not him. Phew. That's when I know how much I want to go. I want to leave, right now.

Mum puts the phone down.

'Come on,' I say. It's me that's impatient now.

Mum meets my eyes. Something's wrong.

'What? Who was on the phone?'

'It's your dad's work.' Her voice is monotone, her eyes strangely glassy. 'He's been taken ill. They've put him in a cab home. They wanted to check someone was here to look after him.'

'We can still go,' I insist. 'He'll survive.'

Mum shakes her head. 'I can't leave him if he's ill.'

I glare at her.

'How can I?' she says. 'How would he manage? We'd better unpack those bags. Come on – quickly. He could be here any minute.'

'But Mum…'

'A few minutes back you didn't want to go,' says Mum, hurrying upstairs.

'Of course I want to go, I couldn't take it in, that's all,' I say, following her. 'I want to go now – I do. Please – let's go.'

'Forget it,' says Mum. She sighs dejectedly. 'It clearly wasn't meant to be. Get that bag unpacked.'

But I don't unpack my bag. Instead, I push it right to the back of the wardrobe. I have this awful feeling – if only I hadn't gone to the loo – maybe we'd have got out before the phone rang again. I put my music back on loud and Mum yells at me to turn it down. I don't want to – but I do – because I hear the taxi outside. HE's back.

Twenty-four

When Leah arrived at school the next day, a group of girls from her class were huddled together by the gate, giggling about something. Leah walked quickly past them but one of them saw her and Leah heard her whisper, 'Ooooooooh Ooooooooh,' in a singsong voice.

Leah glanced at the girl, Chloe, and frowned.

'It's the haunted girl!' called Chloe. 'She's been looking spooked lately, hasn't she? Now we know why!'

The others sniggered, turning towards Leah.

'Are you sure you should be at school, Leah? Maybe there's another *world* that would suit you better...'

Leah walked quickly into school, fuming with fury and stunned with disbelief. Nikki had told Chloe and now everyone knew. How could Nikki do it? How could she? Even if she hadn't believed her about the ghost – to tell everyone else – to let them all laugh at her. Leah couldn't believe Nikki would be that cruel.

'Leah! Leah, wait!'

Leah walked faster. It was Nikki and she was the last person Leah wanted to talk to.

But Nikki ran and caught her up.

Leah turned to face her. 'How could you?' she demanded. 'I know you didn't believe me but I thought we were friends.'

'It just slipped out,' said Nikki. 'I'm so sorry. I only told Maxine. I trust her – I only told her because I was worried about you. I didn't think she'd go and tell Chloe.'

'Now they all know,' said Leah, folding her arms tight against her chest. 'They're all laughing at me – because of you!'

'Leah – I didn't mean to say anything. Don't go off on one,' said Nikki.

'Just get away from me.'

Nikki showed no signs of moving – so Leah moved instead. She was tempted to walk right out of school – she couldn't bear to be there. But it would mean going past Chloe and Georgia and the others, who were still standing by the gate.

Instead, she headed for her classroom and slumped down at her desk, head on her hands.

It was a horrendous day. She spoke to no one and no one spoke to her – they only giggled and 'ooooooh-d'. It was like before she'd got friendly with Nikki – and it made her realise just how important Nikki's friendship was to her. She couldn't believe Nikki had betrayed her like that, so that the whole school was laughing at her.

At least when she got home she found that Dad had pulled himself together. He was working rather slowly, without the usual enthusiasm. But he was working. She couldn't let him see how she was feeling – she didn't want to set him off again.

'Can I help you, Dad?' she asked. 'You know I said I would.'

Dad smiled. 'Here – can you unscrew these? Oh – and Dave left this for you before they went off yesterday. I forgot to tell you.'

He pushed a shoe box towards her from the corner. 'He said you wanted any old bits and bobs from the house but don't get too excited. I'm sure you didn't mean things like this!'

Leah picked up the box eagerly. If only there was something in it – a clue – some proof about what happened to Mark. She scrabbled around. The box contained two marbles, a broken biro, a postcard, a grimy old train ticket, a tiny tin with flowers on it and a Lego brick. Leah sighed. What had she expected – a blood-stained knife?

She picked up the postcard first. It had a black and white seaside picture on the front with 'Greetings from Margate'. She turned it over. The stamp looked very old and the writing was scrawly. She tried to make out the postmark but it wasn't clear. It was addressed to the house – to a Mrs D Tompkins.

'To Deirdre, Having a lovely time. Weather windy but sunny. See you next week. All good wishes, Pam.'

'Can you see the date on this?' She handed the card to her dad, who held it up to the light and squinted.

'Looks like 1949 to me,' said Dad.

Leah put it back and picked up the tiny tin. She rubbed it with her finger. 'This is pretty. I wonder if there's anything in it.' She pulled at the lid, which seemed to be stuck tight. It came off suddenly – but the tin was empty.

'It's just an old pill box,' said Dad. He smiled. 'Now, shall I unscrew these myself or are you going to do it?'

'Sorry – you distracted me with this stuff.' Leah put the pill box and postcard back in the box and pushed it to one side. She reached for the screwdriver.

They only stopped when Mum got home at seven-thirty.

'We'll be cooking in here in a couple of weeks,' Dad told Mum, 'and eating in here too.'

'I'll believe it when I see it,' said Mum, curtly. She clearly hadn't had a good day.

'I've got on even faster with my helper here,' said Dad, giving Leah a hug.

Mum frowned. 'Didn't you have homework, Leah?'

'Nothing urgent, and I wanted to help Dad,' said

215

Leah. 'Cool it, Mum. Come and eat something and tell us about your day.'

'Sorry,' said Mum. 'I've come in and started biting your heads off! Let's try again. How about I put the kettle on? It'll be wonderful when this kitchen's finished. I am really looking forward to it.'

Mum went into the lounge and Leah helped her dad tidy up. He picked up the shoe box.

'Shall I chuck this lot out?' he asked, already moving towards the black rubbish sack in the corner.

'No, Dad, wait.' After the clothes, which he'd thrown so quickly, she wanted to be sure she hadn't missed anything in the box.

Dad looked at her doubtfully but handed it to her. She took it upstairs and left it on her desk, heading back down to join her parents.

Later, when she came back up, Leah sat at the desk and looked in the box again. She rolled a marble and the Lego brick in her hand, the smooth roundness contrasting with the hard bumpy surface of the brick. She reread the postcard and picked up the train ticket. It was so grimy she could hardly make it out. The destination began with an 'A'. The date . . . 21 March 19 something . . . 1970 or was it 1979? Aberdeen – that's what the place name looked like. That was in Scotland, wasn't it?

Her heart thumped hard. How had she missed this before?

As she examined it closely, she realised there were actually two tickets that had become stuck together. She prised them apart. Most of the surface of the bottom ticket came away with the top one but the corner that remained said, 'Child.' She looked again at the first ticket. 'Adult.'

Mark and his mum – March 1979 – that was when they were supposed to have left, wasn't it? But here were the train tickets – the tickets to Scotland. This was the proof. This was the proof that they never made it. Leah held the two tickets, rereading them over and over.

What should she do? Her instinct was to run downstairs to tell Dad – but then she had a better thought. She'd phone the police station, speak to the policewoman in CID.

She found the card with the number and phoned, asking for DC Wallace.

'She's not here at the moment. She'll be in tomorrow. Do you want to leave a message or speak to someone else?'

'It's OK,' said Leah. 'I'll come in tomorrow and speak to her.' She wouldn't go to school – she'd go straight to the police station in the morning.

She went back to bed and lay there restlessly. She wished Mark would come. Why had she mentioned ghosts to Nikki? She'd lost a friend. Her mind turned to Jade. Were she and Megan lying restlessly awake in bed like her? Were they scared of Chris, of what he might do?

Leah finally slept – but woke in the darkness with a strange sense that something was wrong. Her throat was dry. There was a beeping noise. What was that smell? It was like … like … something was burning …

She leaped up, reaching for the light – but it didn't come on. She opened the bedroom door. The smoke caught her throat and she coughed. She could hear the beep, beep, beep of the smoke alarm downstairs. She tried to call out but the smoke got her throat and her voice came out croaky. 'Mum! Dad!' She began to cough and couldn't stop.

She crouched down, where there was less smoke and crawled quickly towards the stairs, still not fully awake. If she could just get to the front door she'd be out. At the top of the stairs she looked down, and felt a searing heat on her face. Panic surged through her body like a burning pain. Flames were leaping up from the hall downstairs, crackling, fierce flames. There was no way out.

Twenty-five

Leah was wide awake now – wide awake and over-whelmed with terror. The only thing to do was to go back – back into her room, close the door and – and what? And wait to die? But as she backed away from the stairs, hand over mouth, a dark shape loomed below her, rising through the flames.

'Dad!' He looked as if he was on fire – but it was just smoke, rising from him like steam. He reached her, grabbed her, held her.

'Leah, I've got you. I've got you,' he said, coughing and spluttering. He turned and looked behind him. 'We can't – can't go down the stairs – it's too bad down there – fire's caught hold.'

'Mum?' Leah asked, eyes closed, clinging to her dad.

'She's out – Mum got out – out the back door. Come on – back to your room. We'll have to try the window.'

She let him pull her into the now smoke-filled bedroom. He pushed the door to but it wouldn't shut properly. Smoke was still coming in so he tried to block the gap with his dressing gown.

'That should give us more time,' he said hoarsely.

They fumbled in the darkness; Leah still clinging to his pyjama shirt, Dad trying to reach the window, stumbling over the boxes below. Would they have to jump? It would be mad – they'd die for sure. It was a straight drop to the front drive.

Dad struggled with the window. It was so stiff, Leah could never do it.

'It won't budge,' he said, still struggling. 'Look for … something – to break the glass.' But at that moment the window gave way. He flung it open. Leah gasped at the cold fresh air that swept in, taking long gulps of it. Dad pushed her nearer. She held back.

'We can't jump. We'll die,' she protested.

'We don't have to jump,' said Dad. 'Remember that talk we had from the fire brigade after … after … '

'After Nathan,' Leah finished the sentence for him, rubbing her stinging eyes. They were going to die – they were going to die just like Nathan.

'If we climb out,' Dad continued, 'and hang from the windowsill there'll be less of a drop. And we can throw your duvet out first so we have something soft to land on,' he reassured her.

Leah leaned forward and looked out. People were standing around below – their faces lit by the light of the fire, staring up – pointing, gaping.

Leah gulped and sobbed – then coughed, clutching her throat at the sharp, bitter smoke. Dad squeezed her hand. Where were the fire brigade? She knew it must be only a few minutes since the fire had started but it felt much longer.

Dad nudged her aside and leaned out of the window. 'The ladder!' he called to someone below. 'Get the ladder – in the shed at the back!'

There won't be time, Leah thought. There won't be time. But moments later the ladder clanged against the wall below the open window. Dad pushed the window as wide as it would go. 'Come on. I'll help you onto the sill.'

'No – you go first,' Leah protested, in terror.

'It's all right, Leah. Someone's coming up the ladder to help you down. I'll be right behind.'

He held onto her as she pulled herself up onto the window ledge, twisted her body round and lowered one leg out of the window, feeling gingerly for the ladder with her foot. One foot secure, she twisted herself further, with Dad still holding her. She barely breathed as she clung to the ladder, feeling her way down with her feet. The ladder swayed and she clutched it tightly. Dad kept his hand on her until she felt someone guiding her legs from below. She could hear Mum, calling out. 'Leah, Leah! Thank God!'

As she felt the ground below her feet, she stumbled into Mum's arms, then quickly pulled away, looking up at the ladder. Where was Dad? He should have been following her. He had disappeared.

'Dad!' she screamed. 'Dad!'

The man who'd helped her down – someone she didn't recognise at all, began climbing back up the ladder but was forced back by the smoke from the downstairs windows. At the same moment Leah heard the siren. Within seconds, the fire engine was in sight, speeding towards them down the road.

Mum let go of Leah and ran towards it, screaming and pointing. 'My husband! My husband's up there!' It was like Nathan's mum – all over again.

The firefighters used their own ladder and a firefighter wearing breathing equipment was up it and in through the window within moments, while the others pulled out the hoses. Then everything went strangely quiet as they waited, hardly daring to breathe.

Leah looked at the flames flaring through the front door and the downstairs windows. The house was disintegrating, it was going to collapse. It was going to collapse in on Dad. Her mind flashed back to Nathan – the skin peeled from his burnt legs. Would Dad be like that? Would they get him out? Would he be alive?

They'd got him. A firefighter was lifting Dad through the window while another, on the ladder, lifted him down. Dad's limbs were flailing about. He was clearly not conscious.

Mum clutched Leah and they clung to each other as Dad was lowered carefully to the ground.

'He's dead,' thought Leah. 'He's dead.'

Paramedics rushed past her. Leah turned to see the ambulance – she hadn't seen it arrive. As Dad lay on the ground Leah thought she saw his head turn – or had she imagined it?

Mum tried to get nearer but the paramedics were putting an oxygen mask over Dad's face.

'Stand back! Please stand back!' said a firefighter.

Leah started shaking convulsively.

Dad's legs suddenly moved, his arms too. He pulled at the mask, and Leah saw he was coughing.

The paramedic spoke to him and he lay still, letting them adjust his mask. Leah felt a flood of relief. He was alive. But then she thought of Nathan. Nathan had been alive – but he had died anyway.

One of the paramedics came towards Mum and Leah.

'You're his wife?' she asked Mum. 'Yes…' Mum looked at her questioningly.

'He's all right,' said the paramedic. 'Passed out up there – must've been the smoke and heat. We'll take him to hospital – check him over properly.'

At the hospital they checked Leah over too. Her throat was still dry and painful but they said she was OK. She sat with Mum beside Dad as he lay on a trolley in a cubicle, still with an oxygen mask over his face. Leah wondered how he was going to take it – how he would cope now after everything that had happened. He'd been working so hard on the house. Would he go back to square one – sitting staring into space for days on end?

They'd been given hospital gowns and blankets and Leah pulled hers tightly round her. She still reeked of smoke – they all did. Mum seemed numb with shock and was saying very little, just stroking Dad's hand.

At one point he pulled off the mask and tried to speak but his voice was hoarse and croaky. Leah stood up and leaned closer to hear. 'I love you,' he whispered. 'I love you both.'

Leah bent forward and kissed his cheek. The smell of smoke still clung to him. 'You saved me,' she told him. 'You got me out. I love you too, Dad.'

Eventually a nurse came to say they were moving Dad to a ward.

'They'll keep him in for a day or two just to keep an eye on him,' she explained.

'Someone left these for you at the desk,' the nurse told Mum, handing her a plastic bag. 'Your neighbour, I think she said she was.'

Mum opened the bag. 'Clothes,' she said, showing Leah. 'How kind. People are so kind. That man – who got the ladder and went up. I don't even know who he was.'

'Do you have someone you can stay with?' the nurse asked Mum.

'Stay with?' Mum repeated.

Leah swallowed hard and felt the pain of the smoke still in her throat. Was the house...was it beyond repair? Was there anything left? They had no home – nowhere to go. This had clearly hit Mum too. Her face creased up.

'I'll take you to a bathroom, where you can have a shower and get those clothes on, while we take Mr Dawson up to the ward,' said the nurse.

Mum looked like she was going to cry. 'Thank you,' she managed.

It was a relief to be clean and even though the clothes didn't fit properly, they were wearable and better than hospital gowns. Mum and Leah joined Dad, who was now in a proper bed on a ward with five other beds.

Leah heard footsteps and turned to see two policemen standing outside the ward. The nurse hurried in. 'The police would like a word with you, Mrs Dawson.'

'The police? Why?' said Mum in surprise. 'Wait here, Leah. I'll go and speak to them.'

'I'm coming with you,' Leah insisted – and Mum didn't argue.

They followed one of the policemen into the empty day room. The other stayed in the corridor, talking on his mobile.

'I wasn't expecting the police to be involved,' said Mum.

'We were called by the fire investigation team,' said the policeman. 'They're trying to establish the cause of the fire.'

'I see,' said Mum, 'and you have to check all possibilities, I imagine? But I think this must have been an electrical fault. My husband – he's been working on the house. I can't see what else. . .'

'In this case – the cause looks very suspicious.'

'*Suspicious?*' Mum repeated.

'It's early days – but it looks very much as if petrol was poured through your letter box and set alight,' said the policeman.

Mum gasped. Leah looked at the policeman's eyes. Was he serious?

'I d-d-don't believe . . .' Mum stuttered. 'I mean why? Why on earth would someone do that?'

'Do you know anyone who might have a reason to wish you harm?' the policeman asked.

'No – no one at all,' said Mum. 'This is crazy.'

The policeman looked at Leah.

She shook her head. Who would do that – set fire to their house, with them inside?

'We'll have to talk to your husband when he's up to it,' the policeman said, 'but were either of you involved in any conflict, disagreements with anyone? Were you being harassed?'

Mum shook her head firmly. 'You must have got this wrong,' she insisted. 'It can't have been intended for us. They must have got the wrong house.'

'We obviously need to investigate further,' said the policeman.

'This can't be happening,' said Mum, holding her head in her hands. 'It's like a terrible nightmare. And after what we've been through already...'

'What you've been through?' the policeman probed.

Mum explained about Nathan while Leah sat biting her fingernails. They tasted of smoke and she stopped.

'Do you think there could be any connection?' the policeman asked.

'I don't see how,' said Mum.

'Your husband's breakdown,' said the policeman. 'In his disturbed state, is it possible that he could have set fire to the house himself?'

'Are you mad?' said Mum. 'Of course he didn't do it.'

'I wondered if he might have started the fire, in order to save his daughter and make himself feel better for not saving that boy, Nathan.'

'That is complete nonsense,' said Mum, her mouth quivering with fury. 'First of all, he's been much better lately and he was renovating that house. It was his pride and joy. Secondly he loves his family – he would never put any of us in danger. And lastly, he was in bed asleep with me when the fire started. We were both woken by the smoke alarm.'

'Which probably saved you,' said the policeman.

'Yes, well, after Nathan...' said Mum. 'They didn't have one, you know. Anyway, he didn't do it. You're barking up the wrong tree there.'

'I'm sorry to upset you by suggesting it,' said the policeman. 'We have to consider these things, that's all. It is a rather drastic thing to do – to put petrol through a letter box and light it. Sometimes these things happen when people are involved in criminal gangs, drugs, and occasionally in domestic violence situations...'

'Well, there was none of that with us,' Mum insisted.

'And you can't think of anyone, anyone at all...?'

Domestic violence. The words seemed to flip a switch in Leah's blurry mind. She suddenly thought about Mark – about Chris Hystaff. Could Chris have done this? Was it possible? But why?

'There might be someone.' Leah spoke quietly.

'Leah?' Mum turned to her, as if she'd forgotten Leah was there. 'You think someone you know could have done this? What have you got yourself into?'

'It's not like that,' said Leah, looking at the policeman and avoiding Mum's eyes. 'It's probably nothing.' Leah hesitated. 'I know who it might have been,' she said. 'A man – his name's Chris Hystaff. I don't know if he...I came to the police station the other day. I told the policewoman on the desk – she took the details and she said she was going to pass them on to the CID – to DC Wallace.'

'About this man?'

'Sort of – it was about a murder.'

'*Murder*?' said Mum. 'What are you on about, Leah?'

'A woman and a boy – Mark – were murdered in our house when they lived there in the 1970s. Chris Hystaff – he did it – killed his wife and son.'

Mum blinked and frowned. 'I think the smoke must have got to her,' she said apologetically to the policeman. 'She's talking nonsense.'

'It's true, Mum,' said Leah. 'The murderer, Chris Hystaff, no one knew he'd done it. He has a new partner and she has children. One of them is Jade – you know, the friend I made in Leaverton.'

'Leah, I don't understand . . . ' said Mum.

'I told the police because I was scared he might hurt them too,' Leah continued. 'I didn't think the woman on the desk was taking me seriously – but maybe she did – maybe CID went and questioned him and he found out it was me who went to the police and now he wants to kill me – and to destroy the house and any evidence there might be.'

'But why didn't you tell me any of this before?' said Mum.

'You wouldn't have believed me,' said Leah. 'No one did, Mum. No one believed me. But then last night I found the proof.'

'What did you find?' asked the policeman.

Leah felt a pang as she pictured the tickets – then

pictured her room full of smoke. 'Train tickets – but they'll have been destroyed. The fire . . . '

'Train tickets?' said the policeman.

'Mark and his mum were going to leave his dad and move to Scotland because his dad was violent,' Leah explained. 'His dad, Chris, told everyone that was what happened – that they'd gone to Scotland. But they didn't make it. The train tickets to Aberdeen were still in the house. The builders found them. You see – they never left. He killed them and just told everyone they'd gone. No one suspected anything. And actually . . . I've just remembered – I saw someone – hanging about outside the house yesterday. A man. It could have been him.'

'Did you recognise him?'

'Not really – I only caught a glimpse. But it could have been. It could have been Chris Hystaff.'

Leah's throat was still sore and she began to cough.

'All right, all right. That's enough for now,' said the policeman. 'I'll contact DC Wallace and find out what this is all about.'

Mark
Leaving - Part 2

It's hard – knowing we'd nearly got out of here – away from HIM. I'm on edge – impatient with Mum but trying to act normal. She says we just have to wait until he gets over the 'flu. He's got it bad – all fever and snot. He looks disgusting and when he sleeps he snores like a pig. But it'd be so much easier to leave now – when he can barely stand up, he's so dizzy. He couldn't do anything, he couldn't stop us. But she won't leave him while he's ill – even though he's got her running up and down the stairs all day. No sooner she's brought him a hot drink he wants more aspirin and he's mad at her that she didn't read his mind and bring it already.

I wonder how many soluble aspirin you could dissolve in a glass without the person noticing. I say it to Mum in the kitchen. We both speak in whispers. She looks tempted for the briefest moment – then she says, 'What? You want him dead and me in prison for the rest of my life? What'll you do then?'

'Can't we say he did it himself – by accident, or maybe we can say he wanted to do himself in?' I suggest.

231

Mum raises her eyebrows dismissively. 'Look, Mark. You've just got to be patient – and you've got to behave. If he gets an inkling...'

So I'm staying out of the way, as much as I can, dreaming about our new life. I go to school. I walk back to Simon's house with him. I tell him. Mum said to tell no one – not a soul, but I trust Simon – I know he won't breathe a word. He looks sad – and I feel mean for being so happy. I thought he'd understand – but then he's got no idea, no idea what it's really like for me. It's not something I can talk about.

He asks, 'When?'

I say it could be any day – and I won't be able to tell him. It'll just happen. We'll be gone.

He asks, 'Where? Will we still be able to meet up?'

I shake my head. 'It's too far – too far to meet up,' I tell him.

'What – another country?' he asks.

I hesitate. 'Scotland,' I whisper, 'but you mustn't tell a soul, all right? My mum's got a great-aunt there – she sends us cards at Christmas but I've never met her. Mum hasn't even told her we're coming in case Dad gets wind of it.'

'I won't say a word – I swear,' Simon promises.

'I'll write,' I promise him. 'We'll keep in touch.'

Days go by. HE gets better – but he's not yet back at work. I come home from school and he's lolling about on the settee watching telly.

'Here!' he orders. 'Turn over the channel. Put it on ITV.'

Not 'please' or 'would you mind' – just 'do it, and do it this instant or there'll be trouble'.

I go over and press the switch on the telly – though I'm sure he's quite well enough to get up and do it himself. I want to ask him, 'When do you think you'll be back at work, then?' but I'm scared – I might sound too eager, give something away. And anyway, it's always better to keep your mouth shut with him unless there's no choice and it's something you've got to say.

'What's up with you?' he demands.

I flinch. What does he mean? What have I done to make him think something's up?

'Nothing,' I say.

'Well, get out of here, then. I don't want you going down with this flu. It's a killer.'

I wish it would kill him, I think as I head up the stairs. That'd solve everything. Then we could stay here – we wouldn't have to go anywhere.

Three more days and he's back at work. Two more days after that and I think Mum's changed her mind. HE's not being too bad – she's going to say she wants to give him another chance. But she can't, can she?

Then one night, I'm in bed and Mum comes into my room. HE's out – down the pub. She puts on my bedside lamp.

'Look,' she says, holding something up.

I squint in the light. It's tickets – train tickets – to Aberdeen.

'Tomorrow morning,' she says. 'We're going tomorrow. As soon as he's left for work. Just stay in your room until then.'

'You'd better hide those tickets,' I say, anxiously.

'Of course – I'm not daft, Mark. I'll slip them down behind

233

the skirting in the kitchen. Don't let me forget to take them when we go!'

I think I won't sleep – I think I'll be awake all night waiting for the hours to tick by – but I do sleep. I wake with a start when the front door bangs. I think it's morning – I think it's him going to work – that this is it. But my clock tells me it's half-eleven. I've only been in bed a couple of hours. HE's not going out – HE's coming in, from the pub.

I hold my breath as I hear him thud unsteadily up the stairs. Mum will be pretending to be asleep. I hope he'll flop down beside her and be snoring in seconds. He'd better not start on her – not tonight.

I listen. It's quiet. But then I hear voices. My heart sinks. They're talking. He's raising his voice. Mum cries out in a shriek, 'Chris, no!'

I leap from my bed and out onto the landing. I'm in the doorway of their room. I see his back – still dressed, leaning over Mum who's lying on the bed. She's struggling as if he's holding her down. I can't see her face. Then I see why – he's got a pillow over it, he's pressing down, pressing a pillow over her face.

'Get off her!' I yell. But he keeps on, keeps on until she's stopped struggling. She's lying still. But he keeps pressing – like he's got to make sure. I need to hit him – I need something to hit him with – something that'll knock him out cold but I can't see anything. The dressing table has only small things, perfume bottles, hairbrush. Nothing heavy. I think – the phone – dial 999 – but there's no time to get downstairs, to phone, to wait for the police. It'll be too late.

I muster all my strength. I kick his legs, pummel at his back with my fists.

'Stop it! Get off her!'

He lets go of the pillow. Grabs my hair tight.

'Ah!'

Mum's hand is hanging limply over the side of the bed. I've got to get help – I've got to get down – down the stairs and out – get help. I wriggle, try to unclamp my hair from his grip.

'Thought you were going to leave, did you?' he snarls. 'You and your mother – go off and start a new life, eh? How cosy – and you didn't think to mention it to me.'

I gasp as he presses his face into mine, the stench of his beer breath filling my nose. How did he know? How did he know we were leaving? She hid the tickets – and she can't have told him, can she?

'How d-d-did you know?' I ask.

'Been blabbing, haven't you? Must've told your mate and he must've told his old man.'

I gasp. 'Simon's dad?'

'Yeah – I met him down the pub. He was there with his posh mates. Said he was sorry to hear me and Maggie were splitting up. Said Simon was going to really miss you and it wouldn't be easy for me – with you being so far away in Scotland.'

I am stunned. Simon – how could he? I trusted him. How could he go and tell his dad?

I find myself being yanked towards the stairs. I try to wriggle away but HE doesn't let go. At the top of the stairs, on impulse I give a sudden jerk, twisting round, kicking my leg between his feet, trying to throw him off balance. To my surprise it works. HE stumbles drunkenly against the banister, letting go of my hair as he presses his hand against the wall for support. I give him the hardest shove I can – and he falls, tumbling down the stairs backwards, clumsily trying to grab the banister but falling too fast. At the bottom, his head bounces off the side wall and then he lies still, slumped against the bottom step.

I stare, paralysed for a moment. Then I turn and run back to Mum. I pull the pillow from her face. Her mouth is distorted, scary, eyes closed. I try to open them. I feel for a pulse. Nothing. I shake her shoulders – trying to wake her. Tears are sliding down my face. It's too late. I know it's too late. She's dead.

I go back to the top of the stairs, and stand there, breathless, looking down at the crumpled heap at the bottom. He's not moving – I've killed him. They're both dead. I'm an orphan. I'm completely alone in the world and I've killed my dad.

The tickets – I think about the tickets. Mum told me where she hid them – behind the loose skirting downstairs. I don't know where in Aberdeen Jean lives – Mum didn't tell me the address – but at least Aberdeen is far away. I'll decide what to do when I get there. I turn towards my bedroom, grab my bag, head down the stairs.

I wish there was another way out that didn't mean having to climb over that heap at the bottom. I'm halfway down, breathing so fast, when the heap suddenly rears up, like a *horse, a monster horse. I gasp, my legs nearly buckle under me. HIS monster eyes bulge out of his face, his mouth open, grimacing with pain and fury. I'm seized by panic. I pray that he's too injured to make it up the stairs. I throw my bag down at him, hard, and turn to run back up, hoping it's hit him but not daring to look. My room – I'll barricade myself in my room. But he's following, pounding up the stairs – getting closer.*

I'm in my room, door shut, trying to push the bed against it – but it's too late. HE's kicked the door in. He's as strong as the Iron Man, the bed swings aside and he's onto me – thumping and thumping me. I try to fight back, to protect myself but I can't.

'You're going nowhere, son!' he seethes. 'You're going nowhere!'

I'm down, down on the bed, curled up, hands over my face and HE's thumping, thumping, crushing the life out of me. I'm numb now, I can't even feel the pain. I can taste blood in my mouth. Then he pushes my head back and I glimpse the pillow coming down. I try to push it off but I can't. This is it – I know. This is the end. I feel like I'm spinning, spinning down a long tunnel – and then there's a light – I'm heading towards the light.

Twenty-six

Leah sat on the floor in Nikki's bedroom and let her mobile slide off her lap onto the carpet. Four days had passed – four whole days since the fire. She was staying at Nikki's. She hadn't wanted to – she still hadn't forgiven Nikki for telling everyone she'd seen a ghost. But Mum was so stressed, Leah hadn't felt like making a fuss. Mum was staying with a colleague from work who lived near the hospital. It was only until they found somewhere to rent and got the insurance sorted out. Mum said it wouldn't be long.

Nikki and her family were being kind. Leah couldn't really complain. The worst thing, the most unbelievable thing, was that Chris had not been arrested. Leah had expected the police to go straight round there and take him in, charge him with arson – and with murder. But days had gone by and nothing had happened. They said Chris had an alibi for the arson and they were still investigating.

Nikki came in. 'Was that your mum on the phone?'

'Yes – she's been talking to the police but it sounds like they're doing bog-all. You know when we went to the police station, and the policewoman was going to pass the details to DC Wallace in CID – about the murder?'

Nikki nodded.

'Well, I thought after that she must have gone and questioned Chris Hystaff – and that was what tipped him off, about me being on to him. But Mum's found out DC Wallace never spoke to him – so now they're saying there would've been no reason for him to suddenly come and set fire to our house.'

'You said he had an alibi, anyway,' said Nikki. 'They must have spoken to him to find that out. And if he's got an alibi, it can't have been him, can it?'

'But I'm sure it was him. I'm totally sure,' Leah insisted. 'And I don't think they've questioned him about the murders at all. DC Wallace didn't do anything, did she? And now they've just dismissed it like it's some crazy idea that's all in my head and it's not.'

Leah gave an unexpected sob and then couldn't stop more from following.

Nikki crouched beside her and put an arm on her shoulder.

'I'm scared for Jade and Megan, I really am,' said Leah.

'Could you phone Jade?' Nikki suggested.

'I don't have her number – it was in my old mobile – in the fire,' said Leah. 'And anyway, what if he was there when I phoned?'

'I don't know what to say,' said Nikki. 'I guess the police have got to be sure – they've got to get enough evidence.'

'Maybe I should get it myself,' said Leah, flippantly.

'The evidence? How?' asked Nikki.

Twenty-seven

'Come on.' Leah's heart was thumping as she went up the drive. A sheet of metal blocked the space which had once been the front door. The whole front of the house was smoky-grey and all of the downstairs windows were blocked. She looked above, where her bedroom window was the only one with glass still in it. If she could get in, would Mark come? Would he be there? She half hoped to see his face looking down at her from the window but there was nothing. The house had a deathly feel – almost too deathly even for a ghost.

'What are you going to do?' There was a high-pitched panic in Nikki's voice. 'You can't go in – it won't be safe, and anyway it's all boarded up.' She came up behind Leah and touched her arm.

Leah shrugged her off. She pressed her hands against the metal grille. It met her with coldness and had no give. She tried to get her fingernails around the edge. One nail broke. She bit at the rough edge. 'Let's try round the back.'

'But Leah...'

Nikki followed as Leah headed round the side of the house. The gate was bolted from the inside.

'Leah, let's go,' said Nikki.

'Give me a leg up,' said Leah. 'I'll just have a look. If I can't get in the back, I'll give up.'

Nikki shook her head. 'What are you going to do if you get in? I mean, the police will have searched the house thoroughly, won't they? Are you...are you thinking he...Mark...might, you know...appear or something – is that what this is about? You want to talk to him?'

Leah squinted at Nikki. She had no idea if Nikki believed her now about Mark's ghost. Nobody else did.

'We need to know where the bodies are,' she said. 'That's the only way the police are going to start doing something. Come on, give me a leg up.'

Sighing, Nikki helped Leah up onto the top of the gate. 'Watch out! You'll get splinters,' she warned, as Leah shuffled along and heaved herself over.

Leah landed with a thump on the cracked crazy paving, and fell onto her side.

'Are you all right?' Nikki called anxiously from the other side. 'Open the gate – let me through.'

Leah scrambled to her feet, rubbed her leg and struggled with the bolt until it finally released. The back of the house was not so blackened by smoke as the front.

Leah stepped between piles of builder's rubble and pulled at the back door handle. The door was locked, which was no surprise – but maybe the fire had weakened it – maybe if she pulled hard enough it would just give . . . It didn't. She looked around at the windows. The glass was undamaged but unless she was going to break one somehow, there was no way in. Hadn't Mum kept a spare key . . . ?

'I think there's a spare key in the shed,' she told Nikki.

'I want to go home,' said Nikki. 'Mum will be wondering where we are.'

'I won't be a tick.' Leah opened the shed and began scrabbling around. Under a pot in the corner – yes, it was the key!

'I've got it!' she called to Nikki. 'I've got the key.'

She came out, leaving the shed door swinging and went straight to the back door. The key didn't fit. Leah stamped her foot in frustration and thumped the door. 'I'm stupid!' she cried. 'It's the front door key, isn't it? And the front door's gone – it's just boarded.'

She was almost crying. Nikki was at the gate, holding it open – expecting her to come through.

'Wait!' said Leah. 'In the shed, there's a spade.'

'What are you going to do?' asked Nikki. 'Break the door down with it?'

'I'm going to look for the bodies. He might have buried them in the garden, here. The police haven't

243

even bothered to look. I'm going to look. I'm going to dig – I'll dig and dig until I find them. You watch.'

'Leah! You're mad! If they're dead – the police will find the bodies. You've got to give them time. They said they're investigating, didn't they?'

Leah ignored her. She was breathing fast as she pulled the spade out of the shed. It was heavier than she'd expected and the ground was harder too. She thrust it hard into the border. A centimetre of soil lifted. She tried again, and again – but the earth barely moved.

'Leave it to the police,' Nikki begged. 'Please, Leah, let's go.'

But Leah felt too caught up, compelled in some hysterical way to keep digging. She tested the ground in different places with the spade, creating a series of small holes in the rough grass, until she found a softer spot. She dug out a few shovelfuls and then the spade clanked. Nikki met her eyes warily. Leah bent down and began scrabbling at the earth with her hand. She pulled out a big rocky stone.

The musical ring of Nikki's phone made them both jump.

'Don't answer it,' said Leah but Nikki ignored her, pulling the phone out of her pocket.

'Mum? Yes, we're fine. We've just gone for a walk. We'll be back in half an hour. Yes, OK. See you soon.'

She put the phone away. 'I had to answer – or she'd have got worried,' Nikki explained. 'Now come on –

let's go – otherwise I'll call her back and tell her what you're really doing. All right?'

'I bet they're here,' said Leah. 'I bet the bodies are here. I can just feel it.'

She pushed the spade into the lawn.

'Leah,' Nikki said quietly – and the change of tone made Leah look up. Nikki was facing the gate, and Leah was startled to see that a man with a grey beard was standing watching, with a deep frown.

'I live across the road,' said the man, by way of an explanation. His eyes half-closed as he looked them up and down. 'I saw the gate was open and I thought that's funny…'

'I live here,' said Leah.

'If you did, then you don't any more,' said the man, stroking his beard. 'I don't think anyone will be living here for a while. And I'm sure you shouldn't be here now. I don't mean to be nosey – but what exactly are you doing with that spade?'

'We're just picking up a few things from the shed,' said Nikki, 'for her dad.'

Leah closed her eyes for a moment, relieved at Nikki's support. She hadn't had an answer for him – not that quickly.

But when she opened her eyes, she could see he was looking around at the holes in the lawn.

'You've been digging,' said the man. 'Look, I don't know what you're up to – or if you really did live here –

but there's rumours this fire was arson and I think the police should know there's kids hanging about.' He pulled a mobile phone from his pocket.

'No – please!' Leah begged. 'We're just leaving.'

But the man took no notice. He spoke into the phone and then said, 'Right, the police are on their way and I'm staying right here with you until they arrive.'

Leah sat down on the grass and began to sob. Nikki crouched beside her and put an arm round Leah's shoulder.

'It'll be all right,' said Nikki. 'They can't arrest you for digging holes in your own garden. They can't even say we were trespassing. I mean, it *is* your house.'

When the police arrived, Nikki spoke up first, explaining that it was Leah's house. Leah started muttering about bodies in the garden and the policeman laughed and said she'd been watching too many crime dramas on TV.

Leah got angry then and yelled at him for not doing anything – for not even arresting Chris. She began to cry again and Nikki made excuses for her, saying she'd been traumatised by the fire.

Eventually the policeman and woman took them back to Nikki's. They insisted on talking to Nikki's parents, who insisted on phoning Leah's mum and telling her what had happened.

'Your mum's coming to get you,' Nikki's mum told her. 'She said something about taking you to stay with her friend Kate for a few days. It's doing you no good being round here, so close to where it happened.'

Leah went and gathered her things. There wasn't much. She didn't know whether to take the clothes Nikki had kindly lent her or just the few new things that she'd bought. She went out onto the landing, wanting to check with Nikki. Downstairs, she could hear Nikki's mum talking angrily. She was telling Nikki off for not stopping Leah from going back to the house. Nikki was protesting, saying she couldn't have stopped her and she did try.

'She's obsessed, Mum, honest. I think she's losing it,' Leah heard Nikki say.

Leah sighed and went back to the bedroom. She left Nikki's clothes and pushed the other things into the bag.

Twenty-eight

'I know you're in a state,' said Mum, as they drove to Kate's, 'but honestly, Leah – digging holes in the garden looking for bodies!'

'They'll find them in the end,' said Leah, defiantly, folding her arms. 'Then they'll know I was right. But it's Jade and Megan I'm worried about – Chris might do anything. The police don't seem to care.'

'And he might have done nothing,' said her mum. 'He's got an alibi for the fire and they have no evidence of murder.'

'They haven't found any sign of them – Mark and his mum,' said Leah. 'And they *did* find the train tickets, they weren't completely burned.'

'But as the policeman told you, just because they didn't use those tickets doesn't mean they didn't travel on a later date,' said Mum. 'The police are investigating. It's a shame that great aunt of Mark's in Scotland died years ago. She might have been able to clear

248

things up. Anyway, if they find anything to implicate this man Chris, I am sure they'll be straight round there to arrest him. And don't think you're going anywhere near Leaverton while we're staying at Kate's.'

'I don't exactly want to bump into him, do I?' said Leah. 'He wants me dead. I just wish I could speak to Jade and warn her – tell her what he's really like.'

'I'm sure he doesn't want you dead and you can't go phoning Jade and terrifying the poor girl,' said Mum, firmly.

'I haven't got her mobile number any more, have I?' said Leah. 'And I can't phone their house or he might answer.'

'Can we drop this, now?' said Mum. 'Let's have a peaceful break with Kate and let the police get on with their investigation. I'm sure they'll find out who started the fire.'

It was relaxing to be at Kate's and cuddling the cats was very comforting. Nothing was said about the incident in the garden. On their second day there, Mum went to pick up Dad from the hospital. He was going to join them and in a few days' time, the house they were going to rent would be ready.

When the phone rang, Leah was in the sitting room, reading one of Kate's soppy romance novels. She didn't take any notice until Kate called her.

'It's your friend Jade,' she told Leah.

'What?' Leah looked up in surprise.

'She's been trying to get hold of you and of course, you haven't answered your mobile. She thought I might know how she could contact you. She didn't expect you to be here! Come on – don't you want to speak to her?'

Leah was surprised Mum hadn't got round to mentioning that she wasn't supposed to speak to Jade. But then Mum would never have imagined Jade would phone her there, would she? She took the phone. Kate went upstairs.

'Jade? It's me, Leah.'

'Hi,' said Jade. 'Bit of luck finding you there! Can you hear me all right? I'm just walking down the road so no one can listen in.'

'Yes – I can hear you fine,' said Leah. 'I've been thinking about you – wondering if you were OK.'

'Yes – but are *you* OK? I heard there'd been a fire at your place.'

'Yes – we got out but only just. How did you know about it?'

'The police came,' said Jade. 'They spoke to Chris. They seemed to think he might have done it. But I can't understand. I don't know what's going on.'

'What did they say to him? Did you hear?' Leah asked.

'They just asked him where he was during the night. He said he was in bed. Mum backed him up.'

Leah sensed a nervousness in Jade's voice as she said this.

'And was he?' Leah asked. 'Was he in bed?'

'No – he was out all day and all evening. He didn't get in until about 4 a.m. I woke when I heard the door.'

'So why did your mum lie?'

'Mum's scared of him,' said Jade. 'He's been acting weird the last couple of weeks – really moody. And it's all my fault – it's because of you.'

'Me?' Leah was finding it hard to follow. She wished Jade would explain more clearly.

'You got my text, right?' said Jade.

'Yes – you said you'd worked it out and I was wrong and I should leave you all alone. I didn't know what you meant.'

'I'd worked out why you were so interested in Chris,' Jade explained. 'I asked him about it and he got really mad. I'm sorry, Leah – I didn't know if he even knew he had a daughter. If not, I thought he'd want to know – and if he did know about you I thought he might want to know that you were looking for him.'

'A daughter? What do you mean?' Leah was utterly confused. She couldn't have heard right. 'It's a bit hard to hear. You're breaking up.'

'Sorry, I'm near the car park, there's a lot of cars. I'm walking round the side, it's a bit quieter there. Can you hear now?' Jade asked.

'Yes – carry on,' said Leah.

'You kept asking things about Chris,' said Jade. 'I thought it was weird – and then I remembered how you were standing outside our house when I first saw you. You said you were lost, but you weren't, were you? You were looking for Chris. So I thought, why would a thirteen-year-old girl be looking for Chris – and asking those sorts of questions, like, *What was he like as a dad? Did he have children?* Then it clicked. You must be his kid.'

'And you said this to him?' Leah asked, in disbelief. 'You said you thought I was his daughter?'

'Yes – I'm sorry. I thought I was doing the right thing.'

'And he went mad when you told him?' Leah asked.

'Yes. He was adamant that he didn't have a daughter. I told him about you – where you lived and your name – in case it rang any bells. I was so sure. But in the end I thought he must be right and you'd made a mistake. That's why I sent that text. I didn't think he was going to go round and set fire to your house! Why on earth would he do that? I was right all along, wasn't I? Is it because your mum never told him about you?'

'You've got it all wrong,' said Leah, sighing. 'I can see why you thought what you did but you were wrong. I should have told you the truth. I wanted to – but I didn't know how.'

'What is the truth, then?' Jade asked.

'It's bad, Jade...'

'Go on.'

'I found out that Chris murdered his first wife and son,' said Leah.

'Murdered? Oh, my God!'

252

'They used to live in our house,' Leah explained. 'I only came to your house because we were in Leaverton and I was curious. I wouldn't have rung the bell or anything – but then you came out. I never imagined that he'd have a new partner with children. I was scared for you but I didn't know how to tell you. I didn't think you'd believe me.'

'Murdered? You're being serious, aren't you?'

'Yes. I promise you. I wouldn't lie about something like that.'

'And I told him your name and where you lived,' said Jade.

'Once he knew my address,' said Leah, 'and that I'd been asking those questions about him – he must have realised I knew something about his past. But it wasn't your fault – you weren't to know. Where's Chris now?'

'He's at home.'

'You and your mum and Megan, you've got to get out of there,' said Leah. 'He's dangerous.'

'The policeman asked me if Chris had been in all night and I said I'd been asleep. He was right there, I couldn't say that I heard him come in, could I?'

'You've got to call the police,' said Leah, 'and tell them the truth.'

'I'll get Mum and Megan out first,' said Jade. 'I don't want the police barging in to arrest him with them there. I don't know what he'll do.'

'Call me later,' said Leah, 'and tell me what's happened. I've got a new mobile. Tell me your number and I'll text you so you've got mine. You will ring, won't you? Otherwise I'll be worried.'

'Yeah – of course.'

Leah wrote down Jade's mobile number and texted her straight away with 'Good luck.'

Jade texted back with 'Thanks!'

Leah's stomach was churning as she put down her mobile.

Twenty-nine

Leah managed to persuade Kate not to mention to Mum or Dad that Jade had phoned. She told Kate she was pleased to know that Jade and Megan were fine but that Mum wouldn't understand. Kate then realised she probably shouldn't have let Leah speak to Jade at all so they were quits and both agreed not to say anything.

Leah waited anxiously for Jade to phone. She didn't. The afternoon passed by. Leah sat in front of the TV, stroking the cats and not really watching. Why hadn't Jade phoned?

'Will you give me a hand?' Kate called from the kitchen. Leah helped Kate to cook spaghetti bolognaise 'vegetarian' style and when Mum arrived with Dad they all sat and ate together. It was a long time since they'd had a family meal around a table. It would have been hard going without Kate, but she was good at making cheerful, light-hearted conversation and the meal went well. No one seemed worried that Leah didn't say much and only picked at her food.

Her anxiety grew as every hour passed. In bed, later, Leah could wait no longer. She sent Jade a text. 'R U OK?'

There was no reply. Sometimes text messages could take a while to go through. But she daren't phone. What if they hadn't got away? What if Chris had stopped them? She'd thought she was protecting Jade by telling her – giving her a chance to get her mum and Megan away from him. But what if she'd put them in more danger?

The next morning, after texting again and getting no reply, Leah tried phoning Jade's mobile. It rang and rang and then went onto voice mail. Leah didn't leave a message. Maybe they'd left in a hurry and Jade had forgotten to take her mobile phone with her. That could be it – that could be why she hadn't rung. But she'd surely have been in touch with the police by now – they'd know Chris had given a false alibi.

'Mum, can you phone the police – get an update on what's happening?' she asked, over a late breakfast.

'I don't want to keep harassing them,' Mum said doubt-fully. 'They'll contact us when they have some news.'

'I'll phone,' said Dad. 'I'd like to hear what they're doing – I want that arsonist caught.'

'It's a terrible thing, Brian,' said Kate, 'after all that work you'd done on the house. You must be devastated.'

'Terrible, yes,' said Dad, but something in his voice made Leah look at him quizzically. She had a sudden sense that he wasn't that upset about the house at all. He was angry, yes – but he seemed almost relieved. He'd come to hate the house too – that's what she thought. She'd known it was a bad house all along – and he'd finally realized she was right.

She crossed her fingers as Dad went to make the call. If things had gone to plan then Dad might have his wish already, and the arsonist could be in custody. But his face was gloomy when he came off the phone.

'Nothing new to report,' Dad told them. 'Their latest theory is that it was kids on drugs just messing about.'

'What?' Even Mum looked disappointed at this.

So Jade hadn't spoken to the police. Leah had a bad feeling. She needed to know what had happened. What if Jade had blurted something out in front of Chris – about him being a murderer? What if they'd tried to leave and he'd killed them all?

'How about it, Leah?'

Mum was speaking to her. Leah hadn't heard a word.

'What?'

'Kate says she'll drive us to a clothing outlet place.'

'It's in Carlinford,' Kate chipped in, 'quite a way but they've got nice stuff really cheap; designer labels at a third of the price.'

'Sounds great,' said Mum. 'We had to grab what we

could just so we had some clothes – it would nice to get some decent things.'

'Yes,' said Dad, 'seeing as my own wife didn't remember my shirt size!'

Mum had bought Dad shirts that were a size too small but he was wearing them anyway and looked awful.

Mum and Kate both laughed.

'I'm not feeling too good,' said Leah. 'I really don't feel up to going round shops.' How could she go shopping – not knowing what had happened to Jade?

'What's the matter?' said Mum.

'She does look a bit pale,' said Kate, feeling Leah's forehead.

'It's just my period,' said Leah, clutching her stomach. 'I'd rather stay here and laze about. You go – I'll be fine.'

'I'm not sure – I don't like to leave you if you're not feeling well,' said Mum, eyeing her suspiciously. 'Perhaps I'll stay here.'

'You don't need to, honest, Mum,' said Leah.

Mum was reluctant but in the end Kate and Dad convinced her to go.

Alone at last in the house, Leah tried phoning Jade again. Still no answer. She thought about phoning the police again herself – but then she pictured the smirk on that officer's face – the one who'd come when she'd been digging up the garden. Maybe that hadn't been her best idea – but they thought she was completely loopy now. They wouldn't listen.

She'd have to go to Leaverton – to 121 Green Road. It was the only thing she could do. Mum had made her promise not to leave the house – but this was an emergency, wasn't it? She'd be careful, of course. She'd just find somewhere she could hide and watch – see who came and went. Then she'd know if they were still there. She searched Kate's pile of leaflets under the hall table. Kate had a car so she probably wouldn't have a bus timetable. There was no sign of one. Leah would have to walk to the nearest bus stop. She knew which direction Leaverton was in. She hoped she wouldn't have to wait too long for a bus.

She grabbed her purse and phone, then hesitated. If she went out the front door it would lock and she wouldn't be able to get back in. Instead, she went out of the back door, which she could lock behind her with the key that was on the shelf.

There was a timetable at the bus stop. To Leah's dismay it looked like she'd just missed a bus and there would be an hour's wait. But as she stood there, wondering what to do, the bus appeared. It was the one she thought she'd missed, running late.

She recognised the shopping centre in Leaverton when they reached it and got off but it took her a while to get her bearings and find Green Road. She didn't want to go right up to the house and it was hard to find somewhere she could watch from, where she wouldn't be seen. In the end, she crouched between two parked vans, with bushes behind her. If someone did spot her she'd just have to bluff about being caught short or playing Hide and Seek or something.

There was a car on the drive at number 121 – Chris's car. There was nothing else to see. Leah crouched there for what felt like an age. A passing dog pulled on its lead to come and sniff at her but while Leah held her breath, the owner yanked the dog away without noticing her. After twenty minutes, she had cramp and was thinking this was ridiculous – she should never have come. Then the front door suddenly opened. Leah's heart skipped a beat as Chris came out, got into his car and drove off.

Were the others still inside? Knowing Chris had gone gave Leah the confidence to go and find out. She waited until the car had disappeared down the road, and then checked in both directions to make sure no one was in watching distance. Then, cautiously, she stood up and emerged from the bushes. She had pins and needles really badly in her legs and had to stretch and wiggle them alternately until they came back to life. She crossed the road, went up to the front doorbell and rang it. There was no answer.

So they *had* left – but for some reason Jade hadn't been able to phone. Leah had a sudden thought. If Jade had left her mobile behind, then if she rang it now, she might hear it ring inside the house. Leah tried. 'The mobile you are calling is switched off,' said a voice.

Why was Jade's mobile switched off? She pressed the doorbell again, lifting the letter box to look in. The hallway looked just as it had when she'd been in the house. But she could hear a sound – a knocking sound. And wasn't that a voice? Or was she imagining it?

'Jade!' she called through the letter box. 'It's Leah. Are you in there?'

She heard more knocking, faster, and a yell, a muffled cry. It sounded like 'Help! Please! Help!'

Leah swallowed hard in shock. Jade was in there, upstairs. She must be locked in. There were more voices – it sounded like Megan was there too – and their mum. Leah walked round the side of the house. There was a small window downstairs with frosted glass. She tried to look through but couldn't see anything. She looked up at the small window above. This was also frosted – it must be the bathroom. Then, suddenly, she saw a hand pressed against the glass. Then more hands.

Leah took a sharp intake of breath. He'd locked them in the bathroom and gone. And this was her fault – all because of what she'd said to Jade. But was he coming back? Leah fumbled with her mobile and pressed 999. She asked for police, gave the address – explained who Chris was. She was reluctant to give her name in case they didn't take her seriously, but in the end she told them, insisting that this was for real.

261

She came off the phone, and looked up again at the window. Someone was writing something on the glass – with lipstick. Leah had to shield her eyes and stand back to see. It was still hard to read from this angle on the frosted glass. Some of the letters were back-to-front.

KEY BACK UNDER STONE

The key! They had a spare key in the garden. Under a stone. Leah gave a thumbs up and made for the gate – which wasn't locked. It was a weird garden, small, with no lawn, just a patio, and there was a pile of large smooth stones in the centre. The top one had a hole. It must be a fountain of some kind. Leah began lifting the stones around the bottom. A huge spider ran out and Leah jumped. She lifted the next stones more tentatively. There was no sign of a key. She was frantic now, and looked around – in case there was another stone, somewhere else. She couldn't see one – so carried on. Yes! A key clanked onto the patio. It looked like a front door key. Leah grabbed it, rushed round the front and fumbled to get it into the lock. She was in. The house had an eerie, empty feeling – but it wasn't empty. She knew that. She ran up the stairs at double-speed, almost tumbling at one point.

'I'm in! I'm here. Don't worry, I'll get you out.'

She could hear Megan crying. The bathroom door had an ordinary keyhole. But the key wasn't in it. Leah's heart sank. She looked around frantically.

'I've just got to find the key to the room,' she called.

'You'd better be quick.' It was Jade. 'We've got to get out before he gets back.' There was a note of terror in her voice.

So he was coming back. Leah felt her stomach lurch. She went into the room opposite – Jade and Megan's room. There it was – the key, tossed on the bed. At least she hoped it was the right key.

'I've got it – I've got it. I'll get you out.'

She heard a car pull up outside and a car door slam. 'Don't worry – that'll be the police,' she told them, as she pushed the key into the lock and turned it.

At the same moment, she heard the front door click open.

'Honey, I'm home!' came a sneering voice from below.

Thirty

Leah pulled the bathroom door open, as the front door slammed below. Her heart was pounding like a hammer. With all of them, they'd surely be able to push past him, trip him up or something. But then she saw them. Jade's mum had a black, puffy eye and a cut lip. Megan was crouched on the floor, whimpering, and Jade was sitting on the toilet lid, her eyes sunken, defeated. Her nose was swollen and had clearly been bleeding.

Leah gulped. She glanced round – down the stairs. He wasn't coming up – not yet. Phew. He must have gone into the kitchen. Yes – she could hear him whistling, the clink of glass. He must be pouring a drink. He wouldn't be expecting them to be free. If they made a run for it now, they had a chance.

'Come on!' she beckoned, in a whisper.

Jade stood up, hesitantly, her face full of fear. Her mum slowly lifted Megan, shushing her. Chris's whistling below had a chilling cheerfulness.

'Quickly,' Leah whispered. But the whistling was suddenly louder. It was too late. She turned – Chris was there – at the bottom – looking up at her and at the open bathroom door, eyes indignant with shock. The little 'o' of his whistling mouth became a teeth-baring cavern, a lion about to bite into prey.

'You!' he roared. 'What the f...You little bitch...' Something glinted in his hand. He was holding a knife – a kitchen knife. Leah thought fast. In an instant she'd grabbed the key from the keyhole, stepped into the bathroom, shut the door and fumbled to lock it from the inside. He was coming up – only seconds behind. He thumped on the door – and Leah thought it was going to give way.

'Coming here, trying to destroy my life!' he yelled. 'Open this door!'

He thumped on it again.

'Tell me, little bitch, what's in it for you? Come on, tell me. I'm all ears.'

He thumped on the door again. Leah's heart was pounding. She didn't want to speak – but should she? Would it shut him up?

'I know what you did,' she said, her voice quavering as she spoke. 'I know what you did to Mark and his mum. I didn't want the same to happen to Jade.'

'You know nothing!' he yelled. 'You're just spreading evil rumours, turning my family against me! We were happy – we had a happy life, until you came and started

265

messing with it. Happy, weren't we, Lynne?'

Leah looked at Jade's mum. Had they been happy? Had she, Leah, messed it up for them?

Lynne said nothing, just stared at the carpet.

'You thought you'd just leave me,' Chris continued, 'just go, Lynne, without saying a word? Well, I don't think that's very nice, do you?'

'Mum doesn't want to be with a murderer, does she?' said Jade.

'And what do you know about it?' Chris demanded, snidely.

'Leah said—' Jade began.

'*Leah! Leah said!*' He thumped the door again and it gave slightly. 'Leah the home-wrecker! She doesn't know a thing – she's off her head.'

'If I'm so off my head, then how come you've hurt them all like this – and how come you set fire to our house?' said Leah.

'There's an idea...' Chris sneered. 'You think you're so cosy in there – but I could set this door alight – and that would finish you off nicely, wouldn't it?'

The memory of the choking smoke, the flames on the stairs, the heat, made Leah shudder. He could – he could burn them all alive.

Megan began to sob. Lynne held her close. 'Let the children go, Chris,' she said quietly. 'I don't care what you do to me. Let the children go, then we can talk if you want. Whatever you like.'

'Come out, then! I'm not keeping you in there, am I? It's you who's got the key.'

'He's got a knife,' Leah warned. 'I think we should stay here. The police are coming.'

There was the sound of a car door banging outside. Then another.

'That's the police,' said Leah, praying she was right this time.

'So you've called the cops?' Chris sneered. 'Well, they won't be able to do much if the place is in flames, will they?'

The doorbell rang. Leah's mobile rang at the same moment. She pulled it from her pocket, her fingers shaking as she pressed to answer. It was the police.

'We're outside the house. What's going on? Where are you?'

'We're inside, upstairs – four of us,' Leah gabbled. 'I found a key – I tried to let them out but he came back. He's got a knife. He says he's going to set fire to the house. I locked us all in the bathroom. I think we need an ambulance – they're all hurt.'

There was a loud bang as Chris gave the bathroom door a final lunge. The wood splintered and it flew open, knocking Jade's mum sideways so she lay across the bathroom floor, with Megan over her. Jade screamed as Chris knocked the phone from Leah's hand with a swipe of his arm, the knife waving scarily in the air. Leah held her hands up protectively as she

267

moved back, against the bath, and struggled not to fall right in. But the knife wasn't pointing at her. He was pointing it down at Jade's mum.

'You're not leaving me!' he seethed. 'Don't think you're leaving me.'

Everything next happened so fast. There was a bang from downstairs as the front door was forced open. Megan clung to her mum. There were loud footsteps on the stairs.

'Drop the knife!' a policeman demanded. Chris lunged forward – forward at Lynne. But Megan was in the way. The policeman grabbed at Chris, there was a flash of metal – the knife. Leah closed her eyes. Megan screamed. It was like an animal cry – the loudest, most ear-splitting scream Leah had ever heard. Shaking, hands over her face, Leah peeked between her fingers. Chris was crouched forward, bent over Megan and her mum. Megan was covered with blood. It spilled out, over her mum. Jade stood by the toilet staring, her face deathly white.

He'd stabbed Megan. He'd stabbed her. Leah began to shiver uncontrollably. Two policemen pulled Chris back but he stayed crumpled, not rising to his feet. It was only as the police tried to lift him, that Leah saw Chris's blood-soaked shirt – and gasped. He had not stabbed Megan – but had somehow managed to stab himself. It was his blood – his blood that was flowing over Megan, over her mum, the floor.

Big hands lifted Megan clear, then Jade, and their mum. Leah's legs were wobbling as she was helped to step over Chris, who now lay moaning in a pool of blood on the bathroom floor. Leah fell into the arms of a policeman on the landing. Another policeman joined the one in the bathroom. There were more on the stairs. They seemed to be everywhere. In the midst of it all, Leah heard the sound of her mobile phone ringing. The sound was peculiarly alien – too ordinary – too real for right now.

'My...my phone,' she murmured. A policeman held it up and it was passed to her. Leah took it, pressing to answer as if on autopilot.

'Leah? Why didn't you answer Kate's land line?' Mum's voice spoke from what felt like another world. 'Never mind. I've found you a lovely top – it's that blue that really suits you. Shall I get it?'

Thirty-one

'You could have been killed!'

This was the first thing Mum had said when she and Dad had arrived at the police station to pick Leah up. Now, a week had passed, and Mum kept on saying it, every time there was something on the news, or in the paper. At first Leah had expected Mum to be furious that she'd broken her promise to stay at Kate's, but Mum just seemed relieved that she was alive.

Mum hugged Leah close, and Leah snuggled up against her on the sofa in the modern rented house where they had moved a few days before. On the television, the reporter was standing outside 121 Green Road, speaking into a microphone.

'This is the home of Chris Hystaff, where he attacked his partner and her children and held them hostage in a terrifying ordeal last week. Chris is expected to be released from hospital today...'

Leah clutched Mum's hand as he continued.

'...where he has been under police guard since the incident, recovering from knife wounds he inflicted on himself as police tried to restrain him. He will remain in police custody and is expected to be questioned further as more shocking allegations were revealed today.

'In a new twist, police are now investigating the possibility that Chris may have murdered his wife and son thirty years ago. At that time, Chris Hystaff told neighbours and relatives that his wife, Maggie, had left him and taken her son Mark to live in Scotland. However, no trace of them has been found. Chris's present neighbours in Green Road were horrified to hear the latest news.'

The reporter held the microphone in front of an elderly woman with a yellow cardigan.

'We're all shocked to the core,' said the woman. 'I didn't know him well but he seemed like a pleasant enough man. You'd never have imagined...Shocking, truly shocking.'

The reporter took over again. 'Police have been searching a house and garden in Finswood where Chris lived in the 1970s.' A picture flashed up of their smoke-stained house as he continued. 'The house was recently badly damaged by fire in an arson attempt, for which Chris Hystaff is also a suspect.

'Meanwhile, Jane Gordon has come forward to tell police about the domestic violence she suffered at the hands of Chris Hystaff during a three-year relationship in the 1980s.'

'There were probably more, too,' said Mum, sighing.

'But Jade said he'd never been violent to them, not before what happened last week,' said Leah. Chris's words had stayed in her mind. '*We were happy,*' he'd said and it worried her – that maybe it was true and they would have carried on being happy if she hadn't told them about Chris's past.

'However he'd been acting,' said Mum, 'he certainly showed his true colours when he beat them all up, locked them in the bathroom and then threatened them with a knife.'

'But he only did that because of me,' said Leah, 'because I told Jade and she tried to warn her mum and he overheard and went ballistic.'

'He might have been keeping himself under control before, but anything could have set him off at any time,' said Mum. 'Lynne is grateful to you, isn't she? Didn't Jade tell you that when you spoke to her the other day?'

'Yes – she said her mum reckons they're well out of it. She said he's clearly a very dangerous man. I wish they'd managed to leave though – without having to go through what happened. It was so awful.'

'It must have been terrifying for them – and for you too,' said Mum, putting her hand on Leah's arm. 'You were incredibly brave. I'm only sorry we didn't take what you'd been saying more seriously.'

'What makes a man be like that?' Leah asked, leaning even closer against her mum.

'Who knows?' said Mum, shaking her head. 'Maybe his own father was violent when he was a kid. I think he must have experienced it himself to turn out like that.'

'But if he got hit then he'd know what it felt like, wouldn't he?' said Leah. 'He'd want to make sure it was different for his own wife and kids.'

'You'd think so, and sometimes that happens, but not always,' said Mum. 'He is clearly a very damaged man.'

'So you think we should feel sorry for him?' Leah asked in horror.

'No – I'm not saying that. People don't have to repeat the patterns of the past. There's always the choice to change. He could have got help if he needed it – not gone round battering and murdering people.'

At that moment Dad came into the room.

'All right, love?' said Mum.

'Yes – I just had a call from the police,' said Dad. 'They've finished searching our house. They say we can go and see if there's anything we can salvage.'

'What, today?' said Mum.

Dad nodded.

'But have they finished searching the garden?' Leah asked.

'They haven't found anything yet,' said Dad. 'There's

a machine apparently, one that archaeologists use, that can detect changes in density below the ground, but it'll be a few days before they can get hold of it.'

Dad sat down, squeezing himself on the sofa beside Leah. 'I said we'd be there at two,' he told them. 'But to be honest, I'm having second thoughts. I don't know if I can face it.'

'Don't worry,' said Mum. 'I'll go – I'll be fine. I doubt if there's much left anyway.'

'I'll come with you,' said Leah.

'No – I don't think so,' said Mum.

'I'm OK, Mum, honest. I just want to see if any of my stuff has survived. Do you think there's any chance the computer will still work? All the coursework I'd done...'

'I doubt it, love,' said Dad, 'but let Leah come with you, Gillian.'

'OK,' said Mum. 'But the garden is strictly out of bounds.'

Thirty-Two

At five past two, Leah stood on the pavement beside her mum, looking up at the smoke-stained pebbledash with trepidation. The policeman unlocked the metal panel where the door once was, and pulled it away.

'Be very careful,' he said. 'We've made the stairs safe but you need to keep to the wall side. Don't lean on the burnt-out banisters – they'll just crumble in your hand. Upstairs is not as bad as down – mainly smoke damage.'

Leah stepped forward.

'Shall I go first?' said Mum, but Leah shook her head.

'Can I go up on my own, Mum? I want a bit of time.'

'Are you sure?'

Leah nodded.

'Well, just be careful then. Call me if you want me. I'll see if there's anything at all that I can rescue down here.'

Leah pressed her hand against the blackened wall as

275

she stepped tentatively up the stairs, wondering what she would find. The house felt dead, eerily dead, and smelled of damp and smoke. She couldn't wait to get out of it again. But first she had to see if anything had survived.

The door to her room was black and open. Inside everything was black too, entombed in soot, as if it was dressed for a funeral to her former life. She ran a finger across the desk and the grey-white of the desktop showed through. She looked around at the sooty unmade bed and her blackened teddy bear who sat mournfully by the pillow. It made her want to cry. Crouching on the floor, she picked up a blackened book. It was her maths textbook.

'I hoped you'd come back.'

Leah leaped up, startled by the quiet voice. She dropped the book.

'Mark?'

'I'm sorry,' he said. 'I'm so sorry.'

She turned to see him standing by the wardrobe, his arms clasped against his chest as if chilled and trying to warm himself. His face was whiter than white against the blackness of the room.

'I was selfish,' he continued, 'I can't believe how selfish. I didn't want to think about the past – about *him*. I didn't want to know when you started talking about where he was living now – about a new woman with children. I blocked it out – it was nothing to do with me – and it wasn't why I was here. I wanted to know about life now – the new stuff – music, computers and all that. If I'd thought anything would happen to you – that he'd do this! Have...have they caught him?'

'Yes. He's been in hospital but he's getting out today – into prison.'

'What?'

'He took his new family hostage and there was a struggle when the police came. I was there. He stabbed himself. There was a lot of blood but it wasn't as bad as it looked.'

'Blimey.' Mark paused. 'Were they all right – the family?'

'Just about.'

'I'm sorry – I'm sorry they went through that,' said Mark, 'and you.'

'They know he started the fire,' said Leah, 'and of course they didn't find any trace of you or your mum living in Scotland or anywhere else. But they haven't found your...your *b-b-bodies*.' She whispered the word and it still caught in her throat. 'I know it's hard for you to talk about...but do you know where...?'

'You won't come back here...to live, will you?' Mark asked, ignoring her question.

'No.'

'Good. I'm relieved. This is a bad place – a bad house.'

'Where did he bury you?' Leah asked quietly.

There was a long pause. 'About two-thirds of the way

down the garden – the rockery,' said Mark, his eyes avoiding hers.

'Rockery?' said Leah.

'You know – the mound with rocks and plants in between.'

'Well, there's no rockery now,' said Leah – 'though there's definitely some rocks in the ground. I found one...'

'Rockeries – they were all the rage then,' said Mark, bitterly. 'Mum would've liked one – but he never got interested in gardening – not until after. The earth he dug up to – you know – well, he must've thought, that'd make a nice rockery. I saw him do it but I haven't looked at the garden since, can't bring myself...'

'Two-thirds of the way down, you said?' Leah asked.

'Yes – on the right. There was a holly bush near it. Is that still there?'

'Holly? Yes – now I know where you mean. Thank you for telling me,' said Leah. 'I know it was hard. I can't imagine what you went through. Do you want to tell me more, about what happened to you? If you do, I'm happy to listen.'

'Looks like most of your stuff is wrecked,' said Mark, again ignoring her question. 'The computer – do you think it will work again?'

'Dad doesn't think so. The smoke and soot will have got inside it, and that intense heat won't have helped. I'll have lost all my coursework for school.'

'I'm sorry,' said Mark, sadly. 'I really am. I did try...'

He paused. 'Try what?' said Leah.

'Never mind. It doesn't matter now.'

'Leah?' Mum's voice broke into the moment, calling from downstairs.

'I'd better go,' Mark whispered.

'No – wait,' said Leah, but he shook his head, winked at her and waved. Then he was gone.

Leah stood and stared at the space where he'd been.

'Leah? Are you all right up there? Shall I come up and help?'

'Yes, Mum. You can come up now,' Leah called back.

Thirty-Three

Leah lay on her bed, enjoying the beat of the loud music from her MP3 player. The new duvet cover felt smooth and cool beneath her legs and the white ceiling was whiter than white – like a blank canvas. The sun was blazing in through the windows. She had no curtains yet which made it even brighter. Two weeks had passed now since they'd moved here and Leah loved the light, spaciousness of it. After the fire they didn't have much stuff – that was part of it, but even so...

Then when Dad had said he'd given up the idea of a renovation project, Leah had tried not to show how delighted she was. She'd seen Mum's quiet smile too. Dad was going to get an ordinary job. She hoped it wouldn't take too long to happen. Then Mum wouldn't have to work such long hours to make ends meet.

She caught the muffled sound of her dad's voice and pulled the earphone out of her ear.

'Leah, did you hear me? Can you come down?'

'Is Nikki here?' Leah called back. Nikki was coming over but she wasn't due for another hour. Maybe she was early. Dad didn't answer. He couldn't have heard. Leah stretched and shuffled her legs over the side of the bed, standing up slowly. She'd only spoken to Nikki for the first time properly yesterday. She'd not felt like talking to anyone at school until then. Once she'd broken the ice, it had gone OK. Nikki said sorry, for not believing her about the murder, and Leah said she understood how crazy she must have seemed. If it had been the other way round, she was sure she wouldn't have believed it either.

There had been a dodgy moment when Nikki started talking about the bodies having been found in Leah's garden. She mentioned the anonymous tip-off that had given the police the exact spot.

'D'you know anything about that?' she asked, looking hard at Leah.

Leah had been evasive and to her relief, Nikki hadn't probed. She'd just said it was good that the police had finally got their act together and had enough evidence, even if it was only circumstantial, to charge Chris with the thirty-year-old murders.

Nikki had also said her dad was going ahead with his school reunion but it was going to start with a memorial service for Mark. Leah thought that was a nice touch.

'Do you want to come over – maybe tomorrow?' Leah had asked tentatively.

Nikki seemed genuinely pleased and had agreed straight away.

But downstairs there was no sign of Nikki yet. Dad must have called Leah for some other reason. She found him with Mum in the far corner of the open-plan lounge/dining area. They were bending over something on the table.

'A computer!' said Leah, as she saw it on the table.

They both looked up, smiling. 'Someone at work had this one going spare,' said Mum. 'We wanted to surprise you with it.'

'And that's not the only surprise,' said Dad. 'Go on, tell her.'

'Have a look at this,' said Mum, scrolling and clicking the mouse.

Leah watched as Mum opened a folder called 'Leah'. She read the familiar names of the files.

'My coursework!' Mum stood back and Leah moved the mouse, clicking to open each file. 'That's amazing! It looks like it's all here. But how?'

'This man at work, he happens to be an expert in data recovery,' said Mum. 'He managed to recover some of the files from your hard drive and transfer them.'

'Really? I didn't think it was possible,' said Leah, 'not after the fire damage. You don't know how much work that has saved me!'

'He said there was one file that wouldn't transfer,' said Mum. 'It must have got corrupted. I made a note.

Here – it was called *My Earliest Memory*. I hope it wasn't important.'

'My Earliest Memory?' Leah repeated, frowning. 'I don't remember doing anything called that.'

'Was it for English homework – on autobiography or something?' said Dad.

'No – I've never written anything about earliest memories, I'm sure.'

'Oh well, as long as it wasn't important,' said Mum.

Leah had a sudden thought. Could it...was it possible? Could it be something Mark had done? Had he tried to type his memories for her to read – because it was too hard to speak them aloud? She'd been frustrated that he'd told her so little – and she ached at the thought of this – the thought that he might have done, and she'd never be able to read them now.

Maybe it wasn't that at all. It could have been something she'd written that she'd forgotten about. But it touched her that maybe it was Mark and he had wanted her to know his story. Maybe, just maybe...